WAR

1

WAR

Two Families.
Two Egos.
One War.

NATIONAL BESTSELLING AUTHOR

T. STYLES

By T. STYLES

ARE YOU ON OUR EMAIL LIST?

SIGN UP ON OUR WEBSITE

www.thecartelpublications.com

OR TEXT THE WORD:

CARTELBOOKS TO 22828

FOR PRIZES, CONTESTS, ETC.

CHECK OUT OTHER TITLES BY THE CARTEL PUBLICATIONS

By T. STYLES

WAR

WWW.THECARTELPUBLICATIONS.COM

By T. STYLES

WAR

By

T. Styles

Library of Congress Control Number: 2018959552

ISBN 10: 194837322X

ISBN 13: 978-1948373227

Cover Design: Davida Baldwin
www.oddballdsgn.com

First Edition
Printed in the United States of America

By T. STYLES

What's Up Fam,

Before I get started I have to first let you know some sad news. Our Twisted Babies family lost one, Almetha "Metha" Coleman, passed away suddenly last month. Metha was a long time friend of The Cartel Publications who never hesitated to go out of her way to lend a hand or show her support. T and I were devastated when we were given the news. When you have a moment, please keep her family uplifted during this time. She will truly be missed, may she rest in eternal peace.

On a bit of a brighter side, you are holding in your hand the novel we've all been waiting for...*War*! First of all, VP of The Cartel Publications aside, I am a HUGE fan of T. Styles and her work. The creativity she has is immeasurable. I could not wait to get at this book once she told me the concept and now it's finally here! I know I said it before, but TRUST ME...You gonna love this one. ☺

With that being said, keeping in line with tradition, we want to give respect to a vet or new trailblazer paving the way. In this novel, we would like to recognize:

MIKE EPPS

WAR   9

Michael Elliot Epps is an American stand up comedian, actor, producer and now author. His novel, **"Unsuccessful Thug: One Comedian's Journey From Naptown To Tinseltown"**, is his memoir on how he found his way from hard times to selling out arenas and movie theatres. Make sure you show him some love and check this hilarious read out soon!

Aight, the business is over, get to it. I'll catch you in the next book.

Be Easy!

Charisse "C. Wash" Washington

Vice President

The Cartel Publications

www.thecartelpublications.com

www.facebook.com/publishercwash

Instagram: publishercwash

www.twitter.com/cartelbooks

www.facebook.com/cartelpublications

Follow us on Instagram: Cartelpublications

#CartelPublications

#UrbanFiction

#PrayForCeCe

#PrayForJuneMiller

#RIPMetha

#MikeEpps

By T. STYLES

CARTEL URBAN CINEMA'S WEB SERIES

BMORE CHICKS

@ Pink Crystal Inn

NOW AVAILABLE:

Via

YOUTUBE

And

DVD

(Season 2 Coming Soon)

www.youtube.com/user/tstyles74

www.cartelurbancinema.com

www.thecartelpublications.com

#War

By T. STYLES

"Blood or not, a family is an organization. Run well and it's highly successful. Look at it any other way and there's trouble. And that's what happened to my family."

- Banks Wales

THE BEGINNING

By T. STYLES

PROLOGUE
FCI LOW - DORM
PRESENT DAY - CHRISTMAS EVE

The room was completely dark as Kirk lay in the lower bunk talking to his girl on a cell phone. As far as he knew most of the inmates were asleep so he was comfortable being in freak mode. He was doing his best to keep his voice down but the phone had been passed around so much by the rest of the inmates that it was raggedy and hard to hear the person on the other side.

"Your fingers wet now?" He asked as he stroked himself to a thickness inside his orange scrubs. "I wanna hear that shit too. Let me hear you slopping around."

"I said yes," Shay giggled. "You must not believe me though."

"Well how wet are they?" He continued as he jerked harder.

"So wet that every time they slip over my button it slides and I tremble." She moaned. "And, and I imagine it's your tongue instead."

"Oh yeah?" He said biting his bottom lip. "I would suck the juice out that bitch too." He continued, as he could feel a tingling sensation overtaking his body, making it known he was about to bust. "I bet that shit sweet too."

"It sure is, daddy," she paused. "Mmmmmmm you got me going hard now. I think I'ma cum any minute."

Getting warmer, his breath increased at the sound of hearing her sweet voice. He felt himself about to explode in any minute, but the pants he wore blocked his movements. He needed to be more free if he was gonna make it work. He looked from where he lay, and when he didn't see anyone staring his way, he whipped his stick out and beat himself faster. So rough he could've pulled it off if he was any hornier.

Normally he wouldn't go so hard but it was a holiday. Most of the inmates were asleep because they were too excited about their visits and the staff at the prison was at a minimal.

As he continued to get his life, the phone slipped on the bed but rested at his ear. So he could still hear her sweet voice and then...

"AHHHH!" An inmate yelled out in pain within the dorm room.

With his dick still in his sweaty palm, he sat up in bed and looked out into the darkness. A few seconds later he heard a thud, followed by several sets of feet scurrying away.

When he picked up the phone he could hear his girl still talking. "...and I imagine your dick—"

"Bae..." he whispered into the handset, eyes peering around.

"Is in my—"

"Shut the fuck up," he continued, cutting her off. "I gotta go."

"What's wrong with you, my nigga?" She said with an attitude.

"I'll hit you back later."

"Fuck you then!"

Unphased, he tucked the phone in his hiding space within a slat in the wall behind his bed. Slowly he rose and walked toward the sound, where an inmate was lying on his side, a puddle of blood under his orange scrubs, dampening the material and the floor beneath him.

After others heard the melodrama, soon a crowd covered both Kirk and inmate #11578. Luckily the prison was old and out of the raggedy camera view.

"This wasn't on me," Kirk said, throwing his hands up in the air.

"I know your green ass ain't involved in no shit like this so calm down!" Byrd said. "Fuck!" He wiped his hand down his face. "This nigga gonna cause us to be locked down all week." Byrd looked up at the camera in the corner of the room that was not pointed down towards the commotion.

"On Christmas at that," Clay added.

"So what ya'll saying?" Kirk asked peering at all of them. "Cause we can't leave him here to die."

"Why not?" Byrd shrugged. "He new anyway. I 'on't even know this nigga."

"Yeah, fuck him, yo." Another said. "I got peeps coming from down south to fatten up my books. He ain't messing shit up for me."

The inmates continued to whisper amongst themselves and then all chatter stopped. ABRUPTLY.

At that moment all eyes looked upon another man approaching the scene. The crowd opened as a larger than life inmate walked through them. He was as tall as a light post and as wide as a building's wall. But more than all, he aroused fear in everyone he came near.

His name was Tops. And many wondered why he was in a low facility to begin with, since his name rang bells on the street for murder. Surely he was better suited for maximum security yet there he was, standing amongst them. Each dead body he dropped memorialized in small dots along his right arm. But the answer to why he was in a low facility was simple. He hadn't been caught for murder...he was in on a lesser charge. Which didn't make him less dangerous.

Tops looked down at #11578. "Looks like somebody gave him a back door parole."

"You...you know him?" Byrd asked.

"Do I know him?" Tops glared. "That's the problem with you young niggas." He pointed a muscular finger in his face. "Stay on the streets but don't know a legend when you see one."

Tops sat on a squeaky bed and everyone else took a seat around him. Many on mattresses that didn't belong to them. An act that would've caused major disturbances including murder if the situation were different. But for the moment the madness seemed acceptable.

"Should we call the C.O.'s?" Kirk asked.

"Nah." Tops smiled sinisterly. "A man put in work for a reason." He rubbed his dry palms together. "He got the right to see it carried through."

Kirk stared down at the inmate.

"Who was he then?" Byrd asked. "I mean, what makes him a legend?"

Tops gazed down at the moaning man. "Since we gonna witness his last breath, I might as well tell the story. But if I'ma do it, it's gonna be from the beginning." He said pointing at everyone.

"Help...please," the #11578 inmate moaned softly. "I'm dying."

"It'll be over in a moment," Tops assured him, nodding slowly. "Ain't no use in fighting it. Go into the light."

Kirk looked behind him and back at the crowd. "We gotta tell somebody."

"I already spoke on that," Tops said glaring at him. "I ain't speaking on it again." Tops looked at the other inmates. "Anyway, he was a member of one of the deadliest families in Baltimore's history."

"Wait," Byrd said. "He was a Lou or Wales?"

Tops grinned. "Guess you gotta fall back and listen to find out."

CHAPTER ONE
THANKSGIVING EVE - 1986

Snow floated down softly from the sky, turning everything filthy, white. Twelve-year-old Banks Wales sat in the passenger seat of his mother's 1982 Nissan Sentra, two French braids running down his back. His light skin, courtesy of his white and black heritage, rosy because the heat was broken and the frigid air had attacked them inside.

Shivering, when he looked over at his mother, she smiled in a way that always let him know things would be okay. Even if their lives of living in misery said differently. They didn't have a lot, but what they did have they cherished, including each other.

"Jingle bells, jingle bells, jingle all the way," they sang.

When they made it to the liquor store, she pushed her blonde hair out of her pale face and touched his thigh. He could feel her cold hand through his jeans. "I'll be right back." She winked. "Think of what you want for dinner and I'll see if I can make it happen."

"McDonalds!" He blurted out.

Removing her folded paycheck from her pocket, she looked down at the small amount scribbled on it. It was only $88.67. Taking a deep breath she sighed. A waitress at a small diner, she barely made ends meet but there was nothing she wouldn't do for her only child.

"A Happy Meal?" She asked.

He nodded.

"I think we can manage that." She pushed the door open and walked into the frigid night.

As she moved toward the entrance Banks was in awe of her as usual. She was an angel, sent from Heaven to look after him. Born to interracial parents, his life wasn't always easy in Baltimore. But she had a way of making him feel normal. Of feeling loved. And so she was everything to him.

As he watched her walk inside the liquor store, he positioned his body so that the back brace he wore, courtesy of fracturing his spine months ago, would allow him the best view with the least discomfort.

After making a few adjustments, now he could see her clearly.

From inside the store, Angie signed her check, slid it to the cashier and waited patiently. When she saw Banks staring at her from the car she waved.

He blew a kiss.

She blew one back.

He winked.

And then things changed.

Suddenly a man wearing a large black coat with a scrubby fur brown hood walked up behind her, making the mood dark. His hands were in his pocket

By T. STYLES

and he looked like the devil. Angie was unaware of his presence but his energy sent chills up Banks' spine. When he moved so close it was weird, Angie finally saw him. But she wasn't worried. He hadn't done anything to her. So she smiled at him once and focused on the cashier as he slid her money across the counter. Instead of leaving, Angie counted it in front of the man, flipping bill after bill.

Right before she put the money into her pocket, the hooded man removed a gun and whispered in her ear.

Banks' eyes widened as he banged on the window with both hands in horror. His breath fogging the glass, temporarily covering his view. This couldn't be happening. This couldn't be happening!

In fear for her life, Angie turned around, her eyes wide and afraid. She shook her head slowly from left to right and the man jabbed the gun into her belly. As Angie handed him the money, Banks could see her mouth to the man, "Please don't hurt me, I'm preg—"

BOOM!

Just that quickly the Hooded Man shot a hole into her stomach and bolted for the door. The bell dinged as he ran out into the street. Wet steps slapping against the snow covered ground.

Taking a bullet belly on, her body hit the floor as other customers ran in the opposite direction of the gunman, leaving his mother alone.

Banks screamed. "NOOOOOOO!"

Angie's focus stayed on Banks, a single tear rolled down her cheek. "I'm sorry," she said. "I love you."

Banks cried out as he watched life disappear from her eyes.

CHAPTER TWO
THE PAST - 1988
BALTIMORE, MD

"*O nce upon a time not long ago...*" Slick Rick's Children's Story boomed from a nearby car radio.

It was a cool day, the type that children adored, but Banks' world felt over, as he looked down at the hole in his white Adidas. From his view, he could clearly see his soiled white sock. He didn't have shit and would never have shit as far as he could tell. And then there was the world, which fucked with a nigga because he didn't have the best. Which is where he found himself in that moment.

His heart rocked as he gazed at the group of fashionably dressed men he had to walk past to get home leaning against the brick wall in the alley. They had history. The last time he bopped past them they took turns yanking off his backpack and pushing him to the ground as they laughed at his holey gear. He wanted to run. Fast. And at the same time he knew it would only make him more appealing for taunts and jabs.

"What you doing, nigga?" Mason Louisville said as he walked up behind him, a forearm to Banks' throat.

"Stop, man!" Banks said pushing him off, dropping his book bag in the puddle of water at his feet. "Now look what you made me do!" He picked it up and slapped at the damp grungy bag.

"I was just fucking with you." Mason said frowning. "Chill out."

Mason was the polar opposite of Banks who was light skin and had recently traded his long hair for a short curly fro. The differences were definitely many. From Mason's dark skin, the fresh white Diadora's on his feet to the red Kangol bucket on his head, this son of a kingpin came from coke money. Even at the moment the pocket in his Adidas sweatpants was protruding because he kept a wad of money on him at all times.

"Yeah well it ain't funny." Banks slipped his backpack over one arm.

Mason nodded and then looked at where his friend's gaze was focused, on the dudes in the alley. Hip to the situation, slowly Mason gazed at Banks' banged out shoes and all made sense in his young world. "Take 'em off."

"Take what off, man?"

"Your shoes." Mason unlaced one of his shoes and then the other.

Banks looked away. "Yeah right."

By T. STYLES

"I'm serious." Mason kicked off both of his shoes and held them in his hands. "You worried about your sneaks right?"

"It ain't like that." Banks pouted. "It ain't like I'm scared or—"

"Not saying you scared." He shrugged. "Now take off your sneaks and stop trippin'. You wasting time."

"What I'm gonna wear?"

"These." He raised them higher and smiled.

Banks stared at him for a minute before looking at the guys again. "Whatever, man." Banks kicked off his shoes. As Banks slipped into his friend's kicks, Mason tossed Banks shoes across the street. "What you do that for?"

"Because you got new ones. Fuck you want with them now?"

Banks eyebrows rose. "So I can...can keep these?" He could still smell the leather of the shoes so he knew they were basically new.

Mason smiled. "They yours."

When Banks laced up the shoes, Mason put his arm around Banks shoulder as they bopped down the alley. The moment the men saw them they looked at Mason's fresh white socks with wide eyes.

"Lil' nigga so rich he ain't even gotta wear sneaks," one of them said.

"Ain't that much money in the world," Motor Mouth responded. "He fuck 'round and catch one of these nasty ass heroin needles." He laughed.

The moment he finished, Mason removed a switchblade from his pocket and went from zero to one hundred. Rushing up to Motor Mouth, he pressed the blade into his inner thigh. Next to his balls. "You got something to say to me?"

"WHAT YOU DOING, MAN?" Motor Mouth yelled at Mason. "I was just asking a question." He looked at his friends. "Ya'll not gonna get this little nigga off me?"

"I ain't fucking with Arlyn's kid," The Second shrugged.

"Let's go," Banks yelled looking around, hoping they wouldn't be jumped in any minute by Motor Mouth's friends. "Please, man."

As Banks continued to watch his crazy friend, his heart rocked in his chest because he knew the violence Mason was capable of and how he got off on seeing blood.

If Motor Mouth wasn't careful this could mean his life.

"Mason, let's bounce!" Banks said louder.

Mason looked back at him and smiled. "I'm coming." Slowly he pulled the bloody blade from the man's flesh, not before nabbing him, which had ripped a hole into his jeans, turning them dark red in the process.

By T. STYLES

"Ahhhh, fuck, the nigga cut me," Motor Mouth continued. "He fucking cut me!" He dropped to the ground, a hand to his inner thigh.

"You gonna be aight." Mason walked up to Banks and put his arm around his shoulder. "We can go now."

As if nothing happened they walked away, the man screaming in the background.

After being at work all day, Dennis Wales opened the door to his tiny cluttered one bedroom apartment. It was such a mess he wanted to walk back out.

"Fuck," he said as he always did the moment he got home, only to be reminded about how poorly he lived. Rob Base's *"It Takes Two"* blasted from a small radio by the window, which let him know that someone was home.

Before walking further inside he stood at the door and took in the terror of his life.

The refrigerator was empty.

The TV was broken.

And people took him as a joke in the neighborhood. At the end of the day he wanted more and didn't see a way to make it happen without knocking somebody over their head for Wales' sake. Something had to give and it had to give soon.

Had it not been for his son and his girlfriend he wouldn't see any reason to live.

"Karen," he said as he kicked off his worn boots at the door. "Karen you here?" He removed the back support belt that he used for stocking boxes at Giant Foods all day and tossed it on the floor.

Yawning deeply, he moved toward the back of the apartment and opened the door to the only room in his place, which he shared with his son and girlfriend. Two twin beds sat in the middle of the cluttered room and it was difficult to get around. The moment the door was ajar; he smiled at his lady standing at the window as she looked outside.

She was wearing a yellow t-shirt and pink panties that made her ass bubble to perfection. There wasn't a bad angle on her body. Her tiny waist, wide hips and fat ass had him sick. Many wanted to fuck her and yet he felt proud to call her is own.

He crept up behind her. "What your yellow ass—"

When she turned around he saw that her fingers were tucked inside her pussy like a pocket. "Hey, I didn't know you were home." She clasped her hands behind her back. Guilt written all over her face. "I was just...um..."

He grabbed her fingers and sniffed. His face turned into a tight glare as he inhaled the scent of her musty juices. "Wait...you in here playing in your pussy and shit?"

"No, I was—"

"Shut the fuck up!" He shoved her to the side and glanced out the window. The moment he did, he saw the object of her affections.

Arlyn, Mason's father, was outside washing his gold 1988 E Class Mercedes Benz, shirtless. Although in his forties, Arlyn didn't look a day over twenty-five. His dark skin was glistening under the sun as he maneuvered sudsy foam over his ride.

"What the fuck is wrong with you?" He snapped. "Huh? You that fucking horny you gotta jerk off to a man washing his car?"

"Leave me alone," she flopped her ass on one of the two twin beds in the room. "Wasn't nobody playing in shit. And if I was it's mine anyway." She shrugged. "So what?"

"Leave you alone?" He stood over top of her. "Bitch, I'm talking to you!"

"What you want me to say? Huh? That I'm tired of living in this cramped ass apartment? That I'm bored to death? That I play with my pussy at least five times a day because I don't got nothing else to do?"

"Get a fucking job! Start there!"

"It's more than that!"

"And what part of this condones you jerking off to a nigga outside again?"

She rolled her eyes. "All I'm saying is this...I'm not gonna stay posted up in this apartment forever,

Dennis." She got up and slipped into some red stretch pants so tight you could see her moist pussy lips whistle. "If you want to keep me then you better start showing me. Or I'm out."

She walked out the room.

Irritated, he followed her just as Banks and Mason were bopping inside the apartment. They were carrying two full bags of McDonald's, which caused Dennis's belly to growl the moment he smelled the French fries and meat. At work all day, he was famished.

"Hey, Mason," Karen said sexily as she walked barefoot toward the door. "Tell your father I said hi." She walked out, feet slapping, ignoring Banks all together.

"Damn she fine," Mason whispered to Banks.

"Cut it out," Banks said shoving him with his elbow before locking the door.

"Oh, hey, Mr. Wales," Mason said when Dennis walked up on them. "My pops bought us McDonald's again. Figured you were hungry so I got you an extra burger too."

"Thanks." He nodded, as he looked at how shiny Mason was with his gold chains. He couldn't lie, although he appreciated that Banks wouldn't have to go hungry, he was tired of being looked at like the neighborhood charity case.

Where was his shiny Benz?

Where were the women who jerked off while watching him wash the car he didn't own yet?

Mostly skin and bones, Dennis wasn't the finest man in the world but he wasn't the ugliest either. The way he saw it, his shortcomings were nothing that a little cash couldn't fix.

"What happened to your shoes?" Dennis asked Mason, pointing at his soiled white socks.

"I let Banks rock 'em." He tossed Dennis the Big Mac. "Besides, I got plenty." Mason tapped Banks' shoulder. "Come on, man, let's eat on the couch."

Dennis sat at the kitchen table and stared at Mason with Malice in his heart as he chewed his burger, shreds of lettuce slapping at the table. He was certain that the money in Mason's pockets alone would be enough to make his closest problems go away.

And as Dennis continued to stare, in complete envy, he realized something in that moment had to give in his life, even if it meant kidnapping the son of a king.

CHAPTER THREE

Banks opened his apartment door and walked downstairs to knock on Mason's door. When he saw it was cracked open, he peeked inside and witnessed Mason on his knees in front of his uncle Gerard who was seated on a kitchen chair.

Banks froze when Mason's head rose and he saw Gerard's penis next to his friend's lips. His heart thumped in his chest as he ran away from the door, leaving it open. Placing his hand over his heart, he tried to calm down while processing what he'd just viewed. Was Mason's uncle having his friend do oral sex on him?

If so, why?

Slowly Banks walked up the steps and toward the apartment across from where he lived. With Mason still on his mind, he lifted a red rubber mat on the floor, removed a key, opened the door and trudged inside.

This apartment was much nicer than his. There was air conditioning; food in the fridge and it was always neat and clean. But what he liked about it most was that they had cable and he could watch *YO! MTV RAPS* to his heart's content.

When he was inside, he flopped on the sofa, grabbed the remote and turned on the TV. Big Daddy Kane was on with his hit, *Ain't No Half Steppin* but he

By T. STYLES

wasn't focused like normal. Banks sat back and watched the video, still wondering what was happening to his best friend.

"Nah...I gotta find out what the fuck is up."

He was about to go downstairs and knock on the door when his girlfriend Nikki walked inside with her twelve-year-old cousin Elena. Something was wrong. Nikki's light skin was flushed and she looked like she'd been running from someone or something. But the real thing that had his mind messed up was her cracked, bloody bottom lip.

He jumped up and walked toward her. "What happened to you?"

"Elena, go to my room," she said.

"But I thought you were gonna help me with my homework."

"I am," she said softly. "But go wait on me."

When Elena was gone Nikki stomped to the sofa and flopped down. Worried, he sat next to her. "Are you gonna tell me something?" His breath rose and fell into his chest.

"It was dad."

Banks ran his hands down his face. "Was it about..." He looked down. "...was it about me again?"

She gazed at him and fell back into the cushion. "Not this time."

He looked up at the ceiling. "Then why, Nikki? Why he hitting you?"

"He got mad 'cause I'm living with my auntie," she said. "And he want me to come home. To be with him."

"You know you can't do that right?" He paused. "He's never gonna stop the drinking, Nikki. Ever."

"You don't think I know that already?" She looked at him and laid her head into his lap. "If only he knew how good you treated me. Then he wouldn't be so mad that—"

"He ain't ever gonna look at me like anything but somebody he don't want around his daughter." He paused. "Ever."

"It don't matter."

"Why you say that?"

"'Cause we not gonna be young forever," she sat up and touched the side of his face. "And as long as I got you I'm good. Love is all that matters."

Banks looked into her eyes.

"What is it now?" She asked.

"If you saw something...or...like saw somebody hurt a friend...but you weren't sure, what would you do?"

She sighed. "I think you should be sure before you did anything." She paused. "Cause what if you're wrong?"

He smiled and kissed her lips softly, her salty blood in his mouth. She was always smart and knew the right things to say. "I don't know how but I promise I'm gonna make you happy you chose me."

By T. STYLES

She smiled brighter. "I believe you."

On a mission, Dennis approached Arlyn who was leaning against his car holding a large Motorola cell phone against his ear as he laughed heavily. Shirtless, a large gold chain hung from his neck and rested against his meaty pectoral muscles. Just looking at him made Dennis's blood boil, especially after catching his bitch jerking off to him from the windowpane.

Still, he had to keep it together.

"Hey, man, can I talk to—"

Arlyn extended a long finger for him to shut the fuck up as he continued laughing on the phone.

Out of respect but still irritated, Dennis stepped back, looked down and waited. Trying to stay busy, he kicked a used needle away and then ran his foot over a can, making it crunch. He felt like less than a man but he had convinced himself that this was for his kid, his woman and his future.

When he first got home from prison he thought he would have at least a year to get on his feet to become a good provider for Banks and Angie. But when she was murdered two days before he was released, he was forced to play daddy sooner than later. Add to that the fact that he didn't really know his son. Banks came with a lot of baggage that not just anybody could handle. If his son was going to make it in the world he needed Dennis in his life. So he stepped up, got a low paying job and did the best he could.

But he wasn't with that shit no more.

"How can I help you, man?" Arlyn placed his car phone on the roof of his Benz.

"I know you don't know me that well."

"You stock groceries at Giant." He folded his arms over his chest and popped his muscles *just cuz.* "You did a few down Lorton and when you came home you found out your kid's mother was murdered for her paycheck at the liquor store around Thanksgiving a few years back."

Dennis stuffed his hands into his pocket. "How you know all that?"

"I make it my business to know the people my son be around." He smiled. "Plus he likes your boy." He nodded. "Banks is cool with me too."

Dennis took a deep breath. "I'm here because I got a proposition for you."

Arlyn laughed hysterically. "Now you overstepping."

"Excuse me?"

"Come on, man." He paused. "Look at your life and look at mine. What could you possibly do for me?"

"It's not...uh..."

Bored already, Arlyn picked up the phone and started dialing another number. "Listen, I'm a busy man. Now I know it may look like I'm out here shooting shit but—"

"I know who you are and I respect—"

He sat the phone back down. "Well respect me by not wasting my fucking time." Arlyn said throwing his hand up in his face.

"I wanted to buy a pack."

Arlyn's eyebrows rose. Amused, he stood up and fell out laughing again. Grabbing his dick he said, "Oh...so...so now you a dealer?"

"Ain't saying all that."

"Then what makes you think you ready for my line of work?" He paused. "Stacking boxes and stacking kilos are two different things."

"I have a family, man." Dennis said seriously. "You said so yourself. And all I wanna do is take care of them."

"But you got a job."

"It ain't paying enough." He sighed. "Come on, man. Don't make me beg." He paused. "All I need is one chance and I promise I won't let you down."

Arlyn nodded. "Okay, okay," he pointed at him. "I'ma tell you what I'm gonna do. I'ma give you some work and at my lowest rate too." He paused. "And to show you I believe in you, I'ma give it to you without cash up front."

Dennis' jaw dropped. "Wait...you serious?"

"I don't play games. You got people to move it?"

"Yes...got family in Texas who knows a few people out here too." He paused. "Thank you, man." Dennis grabbed Arlyn's hand and shook it crazily. "This right here...this gonna put me back where I need to be."

"I know it will." He pulled his fingertips away from his grasp. "But there's a catch."

Dennis placed his hands under his pits and then behind his back. "What's...what's that?"

"I want your girl to suck my dick." He gripped his crotch. "And I want you to watch." He pointed at him.

Dennis' smile washed away slowly. "Wait, you serious?"

Arlyn stared at him intensely.

"My girl ain't a part of this," Dennis continued.

"Then you don't wanna make no money." Arlyn lifted up his phone. And Dennis was so irritated he started to slap it out of his hand. "So step up out my face and—"

"Please, man, don't do this." Dennis paused. "Our kids are best friends."

"Mason got plenty of friends." Arlyn began to dial a number. "He good."

It was settled.

Dennis turned to walk away.

There was no way he could see letting his woman put that nigga's dick into her mouth. Definitely not while watching. And at the same time he was caught between a broke life and his future. There were things he wanted to buy and places he wanted to see. That included giving his son the protection and opportunities he deserved in a world built cold.

He had to suck it up and take one for the team.

Slowly he turned back around and faced Arlyn.

Knowing he broke him, Arlyn smiled and placed his phone down. "So what you gonna do?"

Two hours later Arlyn was sitting bare butt on Dennis's twin bed with the palm of his hand behind Karen's head as she willingly went to work. The crack of his ass on Dennis's pillow, his black dick pushed in and out of her pink lips as she caught each lap, causing long strands of spit to whiten his chocolate skin.

Dennis felt sick in the stomach as he watched the spectacle. Not only because Karen seemed to be enjoying herself, barely coming up for breath, but also because she answered yes so quickly he couldn't even finish his sentence.

And still, he had a soft spot for the whore he hoped would change into a housewife.

When Arlyn started moaning, Dennis turned his head away.

"Look at me, nigga," Arlyn said through clenched teeth.

Slowly Dennis complied, his eyes piercing into Arlyn's dark soul.

And when he did, Arlyn pumped into her mouth so hard her teeth could've shattered. Dennis was trembling with rage. And when Arlyn was about to explode, he held the back of her head with two hands even after she struggled to accept the full length of his dick. He didn't let up until his cream was pouring out the sides of her mouth, while hanging on her chin.

When he was done, she fell face up on the floor while breathing heavily. A smile on her slutty face. Having gotten topped off, Arlyn rose, his jeans hanging off his muscular black ass. He stepped over her, the sole of his dirty foot brushed against her damp lips.

Arlyn grabbed the cocaine off the bed, walked over to Dennis and handed it to him.

"The bitch can suck the hell out of a dick." He looked back at Karen and then at Dennis. "Ain't no denying that. She couldn't be on my arm though." He placed a firm hand on his shoulder and squeezed. "You a better man than me."

He walked out, laughing the entire way.

CHAPTER FOUR

Cars whizzed up and down the street as Banks and Mason sat on the top step of their building eating *Lemonheads* and *Boston Baked Beans* candy. Banks was still rocking the shoes Mason had given him and cleaned them so well that they looked fresh out the box.

Still, there were some things Banks wanted to talk to Mason about. Like what was he doing with his uncle in the kitchen? But before he could, Mason said, "I should take my shit back." His gaze was on Banks' shoes.

In fear, Banks turned to face him and frowned. "Why though?"

"'Cause I feel like it that's why." He paused. "It ain't like you bought them."

Banks sighed. "But you threw my shoes away."

"And?" He said popping a Boston Bake Bean into his mouth. "What that mean? They still mine."

In that moment Banks was crushed.

Since Mason had given him the kicks he felt overjoyed walking through the halls at school. It was the only thing he owned that he felt gratified about and so he cherished them. If he had to give them back now in his opinion his social life would be ruined.

Born proud, at the same time he wasn't about to let him treat him like shit either. So he started unlacing them with anger.

"What you doing?" Mason asked, placing the candy box on the step.

"Giving you back your sneaks." He popped one off and tossed it next to the candy.

"You that mad?" Mason asked taking his bucket hat off and placing it next to him. He knew he had gone too far. "I was—"

"You asked for 'em back so take 'em." He popped off the other one revealing his holey socks, which had a few pieces of wooden shavings on them.

Now on his feet, Banks was about to stomp in the building when Mason said, "I'm sorry, okay?"

Banks had the door handle in his grasp and pulled it open. "Whatever."

"For serious!" Mason said louder. "Come back! You know I wouldn't do nothing like that. You can keep them joints."

Banks looked at him, released the door and sat back down. "Then why you playing?"

"What's that on your socks anyway?" Mason asked pointing at the shavings.

Banks shrugged. "The stuff was on the floor in my house. I 'on't know what it is." He paused. "So what's wrong with you? Why you acting funny?" He was preparing to hear about what he'd seen with Mason's uncle since it had been on his mind ever since he opened that door.

Mason took a deep breath. "My other brothers moving down here."

Banks frowned. "You got brothers?"

"Yeah, a bunch of 'em on my father's side." He paused. "Put your shoes on. I'm tired of looking at your big ass toes."

Banks complied and grabbed his candy box. "You mad 'cause they moving with you?"

"Man, I don't want them living with me." He pouted. "They older and gonna probably be trying to boss me around and stuff."

"Your dad not gonna let them do that is he?"

"I don't know what he gonna do." He shrugged. "He keep talking 'bout how vicious they are and stuff like that. And that they good for business. I'm trying to figure out what that got to do with me."

Banks nodded, not really understanding his issue. He wished he had brothers or sisters in his life so in his opinion Mason was lucky. Before his mother died he had her for support but now it was just his father and Karen who couldn't stand the ground he bopped on. "They gonna help him with his work?"

"You mean selling drugs?" Mason said shoving his arm.

"Whatever, man. I'm not 'bout to say that shit out loud."

"You too careful." He paused. "Well the answer is yeah, but I'on't even care for real. I just...man...I just..."

"What?"

Mason shrugged. "It used to be just us. My father and me. I don't want them moving in and fucking shit up."

Banks looked away. "What about your uncle?"

Mason stared at him for a long time and then looked out ahead. "He dead."

Banks eyes widened. "Who...what..."

"Somebody stabbed him in his sleep." Mason looked deeply into his eyes. "You know what I mean?"

Banks swallowed the lump in his throat. After having seen Mason stab niggas for stepping on his Shell Toes, he knew his young friend was more than capable of murder. "Yeah...I know."

Mason stared into nothingness for a while and then started tossing candy at him. Banks started throwing candy back just as Dennis pulled up in an old cream Oldsmobile Cutlass with paper tags.

"When your dad get a car?"

Banks shrugged. "I didn't know we had one."

They walked to the curb and examined the hunk of metal Dennis used as a vehicle. "Hey, dad, this yours?" Banks asked through the open window.

Dennis nodded, proudly. "You hungry?" He dug into his pocket and pulled out a wad of money.

By T. STYLES

Banks rubbed his belly. "All the time."

Dennis chuckled. "Well get in," he looked at Mason. "Both of you. We going to Burger King and this time its on me."

They quickly hopped into the backseat before he could change his mind.

Two hours later they were headed back home with bags filled with Whoppers and fries. When Dennis pulled up to the curb, he was surprised to see Arlyn leaning on the fence with his arms crossed tightly over his body. His face scrunched up and full of rage.

In that moment the mood changed quickly.

When Dennis parked, Arlyn walked to the car and opened the back door. "Mason, go inside."

"But me and —"

"Get the fuck in the house!" Arlyn snapped.

Mason trembled as he heard the boom of his father's voice. Obeying him, Mason quickly grabbed his bag and rushed toward the door. "I'll see you in a sec okay, Banks?"

Banks remained silent. His gaze on his father. Something about the way Arlyn approached the car made him uneasy.

"Banks, you hear me?" Mason asked.

"Don't make me tell you again!" Arlyn yelled, interrupting the exchange his son was having with his best friend.

Afraid, Mason slipped out the car and ran away, disappearing into the apartment building.

When he was gone, Arlyn closed the back door and opened the passenger's door before easing into the seat.

"Banks, go in the house," Dennis said, his eyes never leaving Arlyn.

"Nah." Arlyn said with a sly grin on his face. "I want him to hear what kind of nigga he got for a father. Best he knows now since you gonna fuck up his life anyway." He looked at Banks. "You staying, young blood."

Banks swallowed the lump in his throat.

"It's been two weeks, man." Arlyn said to Dennis. "So tell me something, where my money?"

"Come on, A." Dennis smiled. "You know it takes time."

"Time?" Arlyn laughed looking around the car and back into his eyes. "You out here buying old ass cars and shit while I'm short two keys? What you 'spect me to do about something like that?"

Dennis peeped at Banks who looked down, embarrassed by seeing his father being treated like an insolent child. "Man, let me get my son out of here so we can talk about it like men. He not—,"

By T. STYLES

"I said no, nigga," Arlyn said as he removed a gun, keeping it low and aimed at Dennis' belly. "Now where is my fucking money?"

Seeing the .45, Banks peed in his pants, dampening the seat beneath him.

"Come on, man...don't do—"

"You hear me talking to you now, nigga?" Arlyn said through clenched teeth. "My money. Where it at?"

When Banks looked down, toward the driver's door, he saw his father's fingertips reaching for something out of Arlyn's view. When Banks gazed harder he saw a broken wooden stick that looked like it belonged to a broom.

Not knowing what it was, slowly Banks stared at Arlyn, whose gaze was still intense on Dennis. And when Banks was sure he wasn't looking at him, using his foot, he pushed the stick closer to his father.

With the makeshift weapon now in his grasp, Dennis grabbed the stick and squeezed, still keeping it out of Arlyn's view.

"Listen, Arlyn, I know I told you I would have your money today but I'm still waiting on some more from—"

"Give me what you got."

Dennis looked away.

"You said you got most of my money right?" He glared. "Give me what—"

Suddenly Dennis pulled the stick up with the pointed edge and jabbed it into Arlyn's belly several times before he could fight back. Not having access to a gun, he had been working on the weapon for a few days by shaving off the wood on the old broom and now he was able to use it. Something he learned in prison. The gun dropped from his grasp and fell into Arlyn's lap. Dennis quickly snatched the gun and put it on the floor under his foot, before stabbing him again.

Banks eyes flew open as he witnessed the violence and just that quickly he knew his world was changed yet again...this time for the worse. His heart rocked in his chest as it became apparent that he was watching his best friend's father die before his eyes.

On maniac mode, Dennis jabbed Arlyn so many times sweat poured down his face, mixing with the red of the blood, turning it pink. Hearing the sounds he made, it was obvious the rage was personal. When he was done, with heavy breaths, and blood splattered on his forehead and lips, he turned to look at his son. The whites of his eyes look larger against his crimson colored skin. "Are you okay?"

Banks nodded although he wasn't.

"Good, 'cause we gotta get out of here." He dropped the stick, threw the car in drive and peeled out.

Under the night sky, Dennis placed the last bit of dirt over Arlyn's corpse. Covered in blood and sweat, mosquitos took turns nipping at his skin for food. Exhausted, when he was done filling the grave, he looked over at Banks who was seated a few feet over under a tree, staring into nothingness.

Dennis dropped the shovel and flopped next to him, mostly out of breath. The sounds of crickets singing in the background. "What you saw today was a necessity."

Banks looked at him, with tears in his eyes. He couldn't wrap his mind around any part of it.

Dennis took a deep breath and put his arm around him, the smell of onions steaming from his armpits, slapped Banks' in the nostrils. "It might not seem like it but you were born into the right family."

"I...I don't understand."

"You're special, Banks." He pulled him closer. "And had you been born to any other family things might have been different."

Tears streamed down his face, as he fought to understand what he meant. Murder and the struggles Banks dealt with on the streets were totally different in his young mind. "Why did you kill my friend's dad?"

"I know it's hard to understand but I'd do it again if it means giving you the life you deserve. A life without question."

Listening to his pops ramble, Banks wiped the tears away with a fist. He was trying to be tough despite being confused by it all. At the moment all he knew with certainty was that his friend's father was gone.

And Dennis was a murderer.

"Does this mean I...I won't be able to play with Mason no more?"

Dennis looked at him and busted out laughing. "I just put a nigga in the ground and all you care about is being friends with Mason?"

Silence.

Dennis took a deep breath. "You'll be friends for as long as time allows." He sighed for what seemed like forever. "But I'ma be real...this, this changes everything."

"You can't tell them, dad!" Banks yelled. "You...you can't tell anybody what you did."

Dennis smiled. "I know." He paused. "*We* can't say anything." He rubbed Banks' curly hair. "What I'll need from you is this...to keep Mason believing that you don't know what happened to Arlyn." He pointed at him with a soiled fingernail.

"But he saw him get into your car and—"

"I know what he saw!" He yelled. "Which is why you have to work harder convincing him that you don't know anything. It's not a request, Banks. It's a demand."

Banks looked away. "I feel like I'm gonna be sick again."

Dennis pulled him closer, his wet onion smelling sweat rubbed against Banks' shoulder. "I told your mother that I would take care of you no matter what, once I got out of prison. And when she died, it was hard at first, considering my past, to take care of you." He looked into his eyes. "It's hard for felons to get a job." He breathed deeply. "But now I think I've found a way."

"We gotta move?"

"All I can say is that I've made a few calls and things are looking up. And even though it may seem dark right now, you will rise, Banks. I promise you."

CHAPTER FIVE

Banks' headache rocked as he walked home from school with thoughts of seeing how Arlyn was murdered playing on repeat in his mind. It didn't help that when they were home, instead of facing the wall with Karen as he did when they went to sleep at night, Dennis spent the entire night facing his son, staring into his eyes.

His life was a disaster.

Banks had been in his high school for only two months after being transferred to another at his own request. So he was just getting settled in before learning that Mason had asked his father for a transfer too so they could be together. Having known Banks all his life, their bond was real and some said unbreakable.

And still, in that moment, Banks wanted to be as far away from Mason as possible.

After looking for him all day, Mason rushed up to Banks just before he entered their building. "Where you been, man?" Mason asked, his gold chain swinging like a pendulum on his neck. His dark skin rosy in the cheeks because he'd been running so fast.

"What...what you talking about?" Banks asked stepping back from him. Wondering if he'd known what his father did to Arlyn just the night before.

"You ignored me at school all day."

By T. STYLES

Banks shrugged. "Why you keeping tabs on me though?"

Mason laughed. "Ain't keeping tabs." He put his arm around his neck, something that Banks hated but allowed in the moment due to guilt. "Just wanted you to meet my brothers that's all."

Banks frowned. "The ones you scared of?"

Mason removed his arm and glared. "Wasn't nobody scared. Just didn't know 'em that's all. But they cool though."

Banks looked at him and then at the building's entrance because he wanted inside, away from his friend's gaze. The guilt he was feeling had him acting differently to his best friend and he blamed his father for it. "Is your...is your dad—" Before he could complete his sentence, Banks ran to the side of the fence and vomited thick clumps of whiteness. His guts pulled on the inside because he hadn't eaten all day.

Concerned, Mason walked up slowly behind him, careful to give him his space. "You okay, man?"

Anything but okay, Banks wiped his mouth with the back of his hand and ran into the building.

An hour later, while lying down on the couch in the living room, Banks heard a knock at the door. Since he was alone he slowly stood up and walked toward the sound.

KNOCK! KNOCK!

Scared, Banks placed his hands on the door and stared at it as if he could see on the other side. "Who...who is it?"

"Me, man." Mason said.

Banks leaned against the door and looked out into the apartment. "What you want?"

"Open the door and stop playing," Mason giggled.

Banks took a deep breath and pulled it open slowly, leaving the door mostly closed. "What?"

"You better?" Mason asked, with a smile on his face.

How is this possible? Banks thought. *Doesn't he realize his father is gone? Forever?*

Banks shrugged. "I'm aight I guess."

"Well come to my house," Mason grinned. "I want you to meet my family."

They were all too loud and spoke of violent things that made Banks uneasy. If any of them got a glimpse

By T. STYLES

of what he knew, would they murder him too, like the man they talked about who had obviously fucked them over for their money on the streets?

And still, Banks sat in the living room with them, nibbling a piece of fried chicken that had been on his plate for over an hour. As he looked at all of them they were as different as night and day.

They were Kevin 19, a dangerous man who got off on inflicting pain on others. Cruz 21, a horny piece of mess that used every opportunity available, to bust a nut in a wet hole. Theo 23, who wasn't as free with his money or anything that belonged to him preferring to be stingy instead. And Linden 26, the genius of the group and the person Banks feared the most.

All had moved from Brooklyn to help Arlyn handle his growing family drug business. Except now Arlyn was nowhere to be found.

As the Lou brothers and Mason talked about a fat butt girl who walked past the window, Linden's eyes remained on Banks. It was as if he was replaying back the murder of Arlyn over and over, even though he wasn't there.

"So how long you been cool with my little brother?" Linden asked Banks.

The room grew silent as everyone turned around to await Banks' answer. Before that moment the Lou's considered Banks to be a non-factor as they waited for Arlyn to come home. But they also realized that Linden didn't ask a question he didn't want an answer too. With smooth chocolate skin and his tall lanky frame, he was a presence whenever he came into a room.

"Not...not...that..." Banks cleared the phlegm from his throat. "Not that long."

Everyone busted out laughing. "What the fuck...this nigga got Tourette's or something?" Kevin chuckled harder.

"Shut up," Mason said. "He know how to talk." Slightly embarrassed, Mason did feel some kind of way that he told his brothers how cool his best friend was and now he was acting funny.

"I asked how long you been cool with my little brother?" Linden repeated. "And I'm expecting a better answer."

"All my life." Banks nodded, as he found himself on the verge of vomiting again. Guts swirling like a washing machine on the spin cycle. "We use to...we use to go to middle school together and now...now we go to my new high school together."

Linden wiped his hand down his face. "Why you acting crazy?"

The phone rang and Banks was relieved that everyone seemed to be interested in the caller instead of him. Besides, the attention weighed on him like a ton of bricks.

"Hurry up and get it," Kevin told Mason as he jogged toward the handset. "Dad got some explaining to do for why he ain't been home."

"You know how that nigga is," Theo added going for his fifth piece of fried chicken that he made earlier. "He probably fucking somebody's wife."

"I keep telling him that one day that shit gonna get him killed," Kevin shrugged. "But the nigga don't listen."

"Hello," Mason said answering the phone. In anticipation of hearing Arlyn's voice, it was clutched so hard in his hand his knuckles whitened. When he realized it was a girl his father dealt with from time to time, he shook his head letting his brothers know it wasn't Arlyn. "He ain't here." Mason hung up in the woman's ear.

"Fuck is going on?" Theo asked. "Where is pops?"

"Exactly, we gotta find this nigga like yesterday," Kevin said. "He supposed to be meeting with Nidia soon right?"

When Banks' insides began to swirl again he jumped up and walked quickly toward the door. "I have to go." He opened it and ran out.

"Something's up with that little nigga," Linden said. "And I'ma find out what too."

Although it was hot outside, and they had no air conditioning, Dennis had to close the window because Karen was crying hysterically on the bed. In their room, Dennis was doing his best to calm down but nothing he did seemed to work.

"But you don't understand," she sniffled. "The streets are going crazy, Dennis! This ain't like Arlyn to not come home. Something is wrong."

"And I get all that." He sighed, trying his hardest not to snap on the bitch. But there she was, his woman, sobbing over a nigga whose dick she sucked some weeks back. "But you not his girl so you shouldn't be this fucked up about it."

"I know whose fucking girl I am." She snapped. "That's the problem."

Dennis flopped on Banks' bed and looked at her. "Karen, you gonna pass the fuck out if you don't take deep breaths." He paused. "Like I said, whatever happened to Arlyn gonna be revealed, but right now it ain't on you to worry about."

She wiped her tears away roughly. "Did you...did you pay him back the money you owed him?"

Silence.

"Dennis, did you pay him back or not?"

"I let you suck his dick," he paused. "If you ask me that was payment enough."

She got up, grabbed one of his shirts and blew her nose into it before tossing it across the room. When she was done she took a deep breath. "I knew this shit was gonna happen." She paused. "I told him."

Dennis frowned. "Fuck you talking about?"

"When he was here I remember, I remember him saying you owed him money before I sucked his dick. So what I did was...was just so you could get the pack. But you still have to pay him his fucking money, Dennis."

"What did you mean by saying you *told him*?" He rose up.

"You know what, fuck it, I might as well tell you anyway." She paused. "I'm the one who asked Arlyn to give you the fucking pack in the first place. And now it's all my—"

"You the one?" Dennis glared. "How the fuck you figure?" He paused. "It was my idea to get that coke."

She placed both hands on her hips. "No, dummy! It was my idea. Don't you remember? We were fucking in this raggedy ass bed and you were talking about snatching up Mason. So I told you to ask him for coke instead because I knew he would give it to you."

"So you was fucking this nigga all along?"

She smiled.

"Wow." His heart thumped. They both played him like a chump and he gave them front row tickets. "You a whore."

"Why you acting all crazy?" She snapped. "Didn't you find me on the streets? Didn't I suck your dick for money first time we met?" She waved her hands. "Get out my face. You sound stupid." She laughed. "Plus I know what you did anyway."

"What you trying to say?"

"I saw you with him."

Dennis' heart rocked harder inside his thin yellow chest. "You don't know what you talking about."

"I know exactly what I'm talking about." She pointed in his face. "You pulled up in front of the house and parked in front of our building."

"That didn't happen."

"And Mason got out!" She continued. "Holding a bag of Burger King food and—"

"You better stop spreading lies, Karen." Dennis was breathing so hard his nostrils were flaring. "You better stop now."

"Arlyn was in that car." She said firmly. "That ugly ass car that you tried to ride me around in. That smells like feet!"

He pushed her toward the wall so hard she hiccupped. "If you tell anybody I'll—"

"What?" She laughed in his face. "Exactly what you think will happen?" She paused. "You a punk! And your kid too."

He smacked her. Grabbed her throat and smacked her again with a backhand.

She placed a cool palm on her warm face to ease the pain. Afraid. Shocked. "You hit me."

"You had it coming! A long time ago!" He paused. "I put up with the way you talked to me, thinking that you would change. And now I find out you done fucked this nigga a rack of times? And ya'll were laughing behind my back?"

"I'm not your fucking dead wife!" She yelled so loud she spit in his face. "I don't owe you nothing. Not even my respect or pussy." She rolled her eyes. "Anyway it don't even matter, I don't wanna be with you no more."

"And who gonna take you, Karen? You old. Your body gonna droop in a year or two and you still haven't learned how to wash your pussy at thirty three years old." He laughed. "You not doing me no favors by being with me. Trust me."

"I'll tell them."

Dennis glared. "Tell who?"

"Everybody!" She screamed. "I'll let everybody who listens know what I saw out of that fucking window." She pointed at it with her chipped nail. "And they'll believe me too." She crossed her arms over her chest. "What you got to say about that, nigggggaaaaaa?"

He flopped on the edge of the bed.

Confused at his mood change, she walked up to him, careful to give him some space.

"Okay, I might as well get this off my chest, Karen." He paused looking down. "It's true."

"What's true?"

He looked up at her. "I did it. I killed that nigga."

She placed her hand over her heart. "Why? Because of me?"

He shook his head. "Not everything about who gets to dump off in that musty ass pussy of yours. Some shit rolls deeper."

She frowned. "Why did you do it then?"

"I did it because men like him don't deserve the money they come by. I did it because I got a son. I got responsibilities and it was time for me to win. And I ain't give a fuck who had to hit dirt for me to make a come up."

"You know they gonna kill you right?" She sat next to him. "His sons just came in town, Dennis. And they gonna kill your red ass dead."

"Maybe." Dennis shrugged.

"Ain't no maybe about it, nigga! It's a promise." She paused. "And I'm not gonna die with you either." She pointed in his face, her fingertip brushing the tip of his nose.

"I know."

"What does that mean?"

By T. STYLES

He smiled at her.

"What does that mean, Dennis?" She repeated.

CHAPTER SIX

Banks had skipped school by sitting in a carryout restaurant all day. He didn't feel like dodging Mason and he was worried that his brothers would jump him while trying to figure out what happened to Arlyn. So it was best to ditch all of his classes and call it a day.

And that's what he did.

Exhausted, and scared, he trudged inside his apartment and toward the room. When he opened the door he saw two, open empty suitcases on the bed. Dennis was seated between them, his face in his palms.

Banks' chest rocked as he figured the school must've called and let him know that he played hooky. And then he remembered the phone was turned off weeks ago for non-payment.

Confused, Banks walked further inside and saw Karen sitting in a chair, eyes closed. "Oh, I didn't know she was sleep," Banks said.

"She not sleep," Dennis said standing up.

Banks frowned.

"What you mean?"

"We gotta go." He opened his drawer and started tossing clothes into one of the suitcases.

"Go get what counts and put it into the suitcase."

"Dad—"

"Banks, we don't have time to talk! Do what the fuck I'm asking."

"Dad, you're—"

"What?" Dennis snapped throwing his arms up in the air. "What you wanna know?"

Banks looked at Karen and back at him. "What's...what's going on? With Karen?"

"I told you a few days ago that I'm serious about keeping you safe. And I'm not letting nobody get in the way of that. Definitely not that twat." He pointed at her body.

When Banks looked at her closely he saw red marks going around her neck in the shape of fingers. "So...so you—"

"Yes, I killed the bitch. Okay?" Dennis looked back at her. "And if she was alive now I'd kill her again. And a third time if she came back for sport!" He shrugged. "Truth is I ain't had a good woman since your mama died."

Banks backed up against the wall and slid down to the floor. In that moment there were so many things he knew about his father. For starters he was a cold-blooded killer. "Why, dad? Why you do it again?"

"You know what...earlier tonight I heard Arlyn's sons in the hallway talking." Dennis filled the second suitcase with Banks' things. "And your name came up. Now I don't know what's going on but we can't hang around here long enough to find out either."

"My name came up?" He pointed at himself.

"Yeah." Dennis paused. "I mean, did you do something to make them suspicious?"

Banks thought about throwing up outside in front of Mason when they had come home from school the other day. He thought about how he ran out of their apartment when Linden stared him down.

So yes.

He had done many things to bring suspicion. And none of them good.

"Do you think they'll like, do something to us?" Banks asked.

"Why you think we leaving?"

Banks looked down.

"Now you gonna get the rest of your clothes so we can get the fuck outta here or not?" Dennis continued.

Banks stood up. "But...I gotta say bye to my girl or—"

"No!" He walked toward him. "You have to leave everything behind. This life is done with, Banks."

His eyes widened. "But she won't say anything about us leaving."

"Son, you can't trust nobody. And I do mean nobody." He paused. "Definitely not no bitch. Don't get me wrong, I like Nikki but now she the least of my concerns. The only thing I'm thinking about is getting the fuck away from Baltimore. And you should be too."

By T. STYLES

The car smelled of piss.

Dennis drove quietly down the dark street. They had been on the road for hours and Banks was swimming in his own thoughts. What would Nikki say by him leaving the way he did? What would Mason do when he realized he was responsible for his father's murder?

Could they ever be friends again?

Banks' head throbbed with all of the possibilities.

Worried, Dennis looked over at Banks and smiled. "You gonna look back at this moment and realize this wasn't the worst thing that could've happened."

"How come it don't feel that way now?"

"It never does, son." He paused. "When you're in the midst of the fire it always seems worse but when you look at your life, when you have more information, it all makes sense."

Banks wiped away the tears that streamed down his face. His father was doing his best to try to make him tough, and to not care about who he hurt, but it was hard. Banks came from a different set of circumstances that caused him to be concerned deeply about everyone he met.

Especially Mason and Nikki.

Not only that, Nikki and Banks had plans. They were gonna get an apartment when he was eighteen after both of them got jobs away from the city. And now it looked like none of their dreams would come to fruition. Dennis' impulsivity had destroyed his world and even in his youth Banks felt the worst had yet to come.

"Will we ever get to go back?" Banks asked.

"Once you make a move this big you never go back, unless the money right." He nodded at him. "I told you that already. Besides, living in that building was miserable."

Banks looked out the window. "It wasn't miserable to me." Banks pointed at himself. "We were going to, going to get an apartment and—"

"This is my fault." Dennis' jaw clenched.

"What?"

"I made you soft. I made you think everything easy in life by giving you what you need, and sometimes what you want, but it ain't that way Banks."

"I just wanna be with Nikki."

"Why?"

"BECAUSE SHE FUCKING UNDERSTANDS ME!"

Dennis was shocked by his son's outburst. In all of the years he'd never spoken to him in such a harsh way. "There it goes." Dennis breathed a sigh of relief. "You got a little bit of me in you after all."

"No I don't."

"Yeah you do." He laughed. "And it rages beneath." He paused. "But trust me when I say this, if Nikki is for you she'll be there when you're ready. But I predict somebody else is out there...somebody you have yet to meet. And you just gotta wait on her, son."

Banks swallowed the lump in his throat. "I don't want nobody but her."

"For now." He paused. "But you will."

Banks leaned his head against the window. His breath fogged the glass and he thought of the night his mother was murdered.

He was tired of talking. He was tired of everything.

When they made it to the stoplight he wished the ultimate. That his father would die, a violent death, so he could be reunited with Mason and the love of his young life.

While waiting on the green light, Dennis looked at Banks and placed a hand on his knee. "You'll forgive me when—"

GLASS RIPPED THROUGH THE CAR WINDOW!

Bullet after bullet poured inside, as the gunmen from the vehicle to the left made it their business to take off Dennis' and everyone else's head in the car.

Tiny shards tore into their flesh as Dennis used his body to cover his only child.

Blood poured everywhere from their wounds and their deaths looked eminent.

And then something happened. Dennis breathed a second round of energy.

"I ain't going out like this!" Dennis moaned as he kept his weight pressed on Banks, and whipped the car to the left and then right...directly into oncoming traffic.

CHAPTER SEVEN
FIVE WEEKS LATER

Sitting in a backyard in Houston, Texas, Banks looked out at the oak trees surrounding the small house Dennis rented from an elderly lady who had been remanded to a senior citizen's facility. Although it wasn't a dream home, it was a long way from the one bedroom apartment they shared in Baltimore. There was space and he had his own room and as a result, Banks could ignore his father in the proper manner.

As Banks thought about his life, he rubbed his fingertips over the gunshot on his left cheek, which caused some of his words to drag. It gave him a mystic voice when he talked but didn't adjust how handsome he was in the least. What it did, however, was give him a scar for life.

After they were shot at, Banks was sure they would die but luckily for the Wales', a policeman arrived on the scene just before the men could finish what they set out to do.

To that day they didn't know who was responsible.

Although Banks was certain they would soon find out.

A few minutes later Dennis hobbled outside using a cane. He was hit in the thigh, which altered forever how he walked. "How you doing?"

Banks looked at him and back into the yard.

"It's been weeks, Banks." He moved closer. "When you gonna forgive me?"

"I'm not mad at you, dad." Banks sighed deeply. "Just ain't got a lot to say that's all."

"What can I do to change your mind?"

"When am I going back to school?"

"You been doing the workbooks I bought you? The math and the reading ones?"

Banks frowned. "Yeah but that ain't enough. I can't get no education like that."

"I'll keep working with you like I been doing." He paused. "Between the books and me you'll be fine. But I gotta be honest; you ain't going back to school. Not now...and maybe not ever."

Banks sighed, having already known the answer. "Where you been?"

"Told you I was gonna be gone for a couple of days. Now I'm back."

"How long we gonna be here?" Banks paused. "Is this *really* our new life?"

"Are you *really* still thinking about Baltimore? Even after everything we gone through? Can't you see when you not wanted? Somebody tried to kill us, son. You and I both know it was the Lou's."

"Not really. Never saw their faces."

Dennis smiled. "You know what...I have a surprise." He paused. "And I can't keep faking like I don't have something I know will make you feel better."

Banks looked up at him. "What you talking about?"

"Come with me."

Dennis moved carefully into the house, with Banks following him suspiciously. Not knowing what his father had planned, his young heart stopped when he saw Nikki sitting on the sofa crying uncontrollably.

Confused, he rushed up to her and she jumped, the moment his cool hands brushed her yellow thighs. Seeing her pain, Banks glared up at Dennis. "What you do to her?"

"I'll leave you two alone," Dennis winked, before turning to walk away.

When he was gone Banks looked at her, making sure she wasn't physically hurt. "Nikki, why you here? Are you okay?"

"Ask your father!" She sniffled, wiping her tears away, leaving temporary red bruises on her cheeks.

"I don't know what's going on." He said. "You gotta tell me something."

"He fucking kidnapped me!" She yelled. "I was walking home from school and he...why did he do that, Banks?"

"I don't know, Nik but I promise I didn't have nothing to do with this shit." He paused. "I would never wanna see you cry. You know that 'bout me."

"Then why did he take me? Huh? And who gonna take care of my lil' cousin?" She paused. "You know how much she needs me. You know my aunt on that shit in them streets. And my good aunt be at work too much to care for her. I thought you loved me, Banks!"

Banks flopped back in the couch.

Once again his father proceeded to fuck up his world majorly. Yes he wanted to see Nikki. Yes he thought about her every time he blinked. But he never wanted her hurt. He had no idea how far his father would go to see him happy. But he realized he had better learn to understand Dennis' vicious capabilities soon.

"I'll call your other aunt and maybe she can come get you," Banks said. "That way—"

"No!" She yelled quickly. "He told me, he told me I couldn't leave or he would hurt my cousin."

He frowned. "He wouldn't do that."

She sniffled a few times and stared at him for what seemed like forever. "Would he? How do you really no? Look at what he already did, Banks."

Silence.

"Everybody talking back home," she continued. "They saying your father killed Arlyn. Is that true?"

He swallowed the lump in his throat. "No."

"Then why you here? Hiding?" She looked around. "And where is this place?"

Banks sighed. "My father bought it after we got here." He paused. "Somebody shot at us and—"

"Heard about that too."

His eyebrows rose. "Are you serious?"

"Everybody saying it was the Lou's. And that there's more where that came from."

Banks looked away. "You seen...uh...you seen Mason?"

"Yeah. But he different now."

"How?"

"Meaner."

"Like that's possible."

"I'm serious, Banks. He could always be crazy but now...now the stuff he doing ain't like him. It's like he's trying to make up for something."

"He'll be aight." He thought about what he saw happening between Mason and his uncle. If he got over sexual abuse he felt he was strong enough to get over everything. "He always be."

"I don't know him good enough to say that."

"What his brothers saying about me?"

"They asked me one time if I heard from you. I kept telling them no because it was the truth, but they didn't believe me. And Mason hung in the background not saying nothing. Just looking. Like he was waiting for them to hurt me to get revenge on you." She paused. "I'm telling you...Mason ain't looking good no more."

Dennis walked back into the living room. "I have to talk to you for a minute, son."

Banks got up and walked toward him before following him into the backyard.

"Dad, why you take her?" He stepped close to him. Chest rising and falling violently.

"Are you really asking me that? The way you been 'round here crying for that girl?"

"Even if you say you did it for me, why scare her? Talking about you'd hurt her little cousin and stuff."

"Because I will. Don't you know me by now?"

Banks stepped back. He didn't. "I don't want her like this."

"So you willing to be with just me? For years? In this house alone while I figure it out?"

"So we really are gonna be here forever?"

"I told you the world as you know it is gone and that's what I meant."

"Well she wants to go home."

"We can't have that either." He paused. "Besides, I called you out here to say I have to make a run. She'll keep you company while I'm gone."

"Where you going this time?"

"I've been asking around the city for some important info and I think it's finally come back. I have to meet someone in a few."

By T. STYLES

"I thought you said not to trust anybody."

"I'll be back, Banks." He looked toward the house. "Don't do nothing I wouldn't do unless it's fun." He winked and walked away.

Dennis walked outside of the house.

The moment he crossed the threshold, a black bag was slammed down over his head from behind. He was yanked, kicking and screaming before being thrown into the back of a van.

His cane resting on the curb.

CHAPTER EIGHT

Mason sat in the living room...dazed.

Ever since his father had gone missing weeks ago, his world didn't seem normal. Arlyn wasn't the most paternal nigga in the group but at least there was structure when he was around. A routine. And now all that had changed.

Little things that he never had to worry about were now his sole responsibility. Like going to the grocery store. Making sure he didn't sleep too late in the morning and always being aware of his surroundings.

When he heard some girls cackling outside, he stood up and walked toward the window. From below he saw Elena, Nikki's little cousin laughing with three of her friends. Ever since Nikki went missing a few days ago, he wondered if she knew more then she let on to his brothers when they questioned her about Dennis and Banks' whereabouts.

When the front door opened he turned around. His brothers Kevin, Theo and Linden poured inside. They were heavy in conversation and he sat back on the sofa and listened carefully at what was being said. In case they had updates on Arlyn.

"I don't give a fuck!" Kevin yelled locking the door. "I say we go up in the bitch and start getting some answers. I don't care who we hit!"

"You can't go up in the projects shooting niggas without direction," Linden advised. "If that's the final move then so be it but right now we have to be smart. We have to be sure."

"That's easy for you to say." Kevin walked to the fridge and grabbed a beer. "You never liked him in the first place." He pointed it at him.

"I never said I didn't like pops." Linden sat next to Mason on the sofa. "I said he wasn't no real man for leaving his sons to a mother he knew was getting high." He pointed at him. "There's a difference."

"Mason's mother was getting high too," Kevin said. "And he don't feel the same way you do."

Linden looked at Mason. "Well he still a kid." He paused. "And he got to know his moms before she hit the streets. Shit's different. Our lives different."

Theo opened the fridge and peered inside. "Hold up...who the fuck ate my food?"

Linden waved him off and focused back on Mason. "You speak to that little nigga yet?" He paused. "Talking about Banks."

"I know who you talking about," Mason frowned. "And the answer is no so stop asking me."

Linden's eyes narrowed. "How come I don't believe you?"

All of the brothers looked at Mason and waited for an answer.

"I don't know why you don't believe me." He shrugged. "If I'da seen him I woulda said something by now."

"Maybe its cause he still think his friend ain't have shit to do with pops going missing," Kevin interjected walking up to the couch, staring down at Mason. "Ain't that right, young blood?"

Mason looked down at his fingertips and then adjusted the chain on his neck. Everything about what his brothers were saying was foreign. He couldn't say much about Dennis, but he knew Banks could never be capable of hurting his father. At least he hoped so.

When his stomach growled everyone laughed...except Linden.

"You scared, lil' nigga?" Linden asked. "How I know you ain't have something to do with pops going missing?"

Everyone laughed.

"Leave me alone." Mason got up and stormed toward the kitchen. "I'm hungry that's all." He took out peanut butter and jelly after opening and closing cabinet doors.

Linden walked up behind him. "I know you scared."

"I'm not scared." He smeared peanut butter on the butt end of the bread and sat it on the counter. "Just don't like people fucking with me that's all."

"If I say you scared, lil' nigga, you scared." Linden said breathing down on him. "Least that's how you acting anyway."

Mason spread jelly on his other bread slice. "Just get out my face. I don't like when people mess with me."

"We ain't people," Linden said. "We family. And we trying to find out where your father is. You'd think you'd be—"

Suddenly Cruz walked from the back of the apartment wearing nothing but his jeans and a t-shirt. A fat butt teenager followed and everybody paused to look at her ass jiggle, as Cruz walked her out the door.

When she was gone Kevin said, "Your dick gonna fall off one of these days."

Cruz shrugged. "Then I guess it would've lived a good life." He looked down and gripped his dick.

Everyone laughed...except Linden and Mason.

"Any word on dad?" He rubbed his belly, walked into the kitchen, and snatched the sandwich Mason just made.

Mason wasn't hungry anyway. Just using the act as a way to get from up under Linden's penetrating stares.

"Nah...but we got some ideas," Linden said looking at Mason harder.

"Well I just found out they in Texas," Cruz said talking with his mouth full of food. "Dennis and

Banks. Some niggas tried to hit they heads but missed. Lucky ass mothafuckas."

Everyone stopped and stared at Cruz.

Linden moved closer to him. "What you talking about?"

"I thought ya'll knew they were down south." Cruz shrugged. "Everybody else did."

Theo slapped the food from his hand.

"What the fuck?" Cruz said picking the sandwich up off the floor and taking another bite. No dust off.

"When did you find out?" Theo said. "And why the fuck you just telling us now?!"

"I just got word today." Cruz responded, looking at his brothers who were now surrounding him. "Like I said I...I assumed ya'll knew."

"They got any idea on who it was?" Linden asked. "That missed the hit on Dennis?"

"Nah." He chewed with a mouth full. "But word on the street is he got somebody wrong. Looks like our dirty work will be done for us after all."

Linden frowned. "FUCK!"

"What's wrong with you now?" Kevin asked. "The nigga gonna get dealt with. Ain't that what we want?"

"I don't like nobody else doing my work."

"As long as the nigga dead I don't care who does it," Kevin said drinking the rest of his beer.

"You ain't dead unless your body washes up," Linden responded looking at all of his brothers closely.

By T. STYLES

"So as far as I'm concerned the nigga still walking unless I see the blood pour out his skull myself."

CHAPTER NINE

Dennis's breath was heavy as he breathed inside the black cloth over his face. He didn't know who snatched him and that made him more nervous. Where was he? To make matters worse, the bag was pitch black and he couldn't see out of it but he was certain that was his abductor's purpose. The only indication that it may be daytime was the little light that peeked in from the bottom of the bag.

But who was trying to hurt him?

"You hungry?" A male voice asked calmly.

Dennis immediately breathed harder, the bag being sucked in and out of his nostrils with each pull. "Who are you?" He asked nervously. "I...I wanna know where I am."

"You not answering my question."

Dennis nodded and swallowed the dryness in his throat. "I'm...thirs...I'm thirsty."

Footsteps sounded off before disappearing. Minutes later they returned and Dennis's breathing increased again. When the mask was removed, Dennis' eyes hurt so badly they burned, due to the light coming from the windows. He had been in darkness for over twenty-four hours.

Able to breathe fully, cool air rushed into his nostrils.

By T. STYLES

A large white man with red pimples throughout his face was before him. He was wearing a pair of soiled blue jeans and a sweaty white t-shirt that was tucked inside his pants.

He was also holding a large glass of ice water. "Here."

Dennis looked down. "I can't use my hands."

The man walked behind him and removed one wrist from its bind. "Here."

Dennis took the cup but looked inside of it carefully, examining its contents.

"If I wanted to kill you, you'd be dead by now." The man announced.

Dennis reasoned he was correct and drank the water slowly at first until he realized how thirsty he truly was. An ice cube stabbing at the left side of his mouth. He didn't even come up for air until the water was completely gone. Placing the empty glass on the floor at his feet, he looked around and took a deep breath.

He was in a large unfinished basement that he didn't recognize.

"Can you tell me what this is about?" Dennis asked, ice cube on his tongue.

The man smiled and walked away.

"Hello!" Dennis yelled at him. "Talk to me! Tell me something!"

Three hours later, two black men in their thirties entered the basement. One was holding a wooden chair. When the tallest man placed a chair directly in front of Dennis, and the shortest man took a seat, Dennis knew who was in charge.

"My name is Gary," he said with a smile. "What's your name?"

Dennis frowned. "Wait, don't you know who I am?" He yelled. "You fucking kidnapped me from—"

The hate was smacked from Dennis' tongue by the taller man.

Using his free hand, Dennis rubbed his raw quivering bottom lip.

"What's your name?" Gary repeated.

"I'm...D...Dennis." He trembled.

"Wow," he smiled slapping his leg. "That's ironic!"

"Why you say that?" He frowned.

"You know, I had a good friend named Dennis some time back. The man spent all day in his boxers, even when he was outside." He laughed. "It used to drive us crazy. We were roommates you know?"

Dennis cracked a fake smile. But for real he was both annoyed and confused at the same damn time.

"But I liked him," Gary's smile wiped away. "I hope I'll come to like you too."

Dennis swallowed the lump in his throat.

"You killed someone who meant a lot to me and my friends." He crossed his legs. "Why you do that?"

Dennis's eyes widened. Now he knew what this was about. His having murdered Arlyn in cold blood as if he were a vampire with a wooden stick. "I don't know—"

The lie was smacked from his bottom lip again by the standing man.

Gary smiled. "Why did you do that?"

Dennis looked down and took a deep breath. There was no use in lying or in getting bitch slapped. It was obvious they knew everything he was trying to keep secret. "I couldn't pay him back. Without paying off my bills too."

Gary nodded. "I can understand that." He paused. "You have a child too. A boy." He leaned closer. "Is that correct?"

Dennis nodded as his blood pumped through his body. "Please don't hurt him." He looked at both of the men with pleading eyes. "He didn't know anything about this. He's just a kid."

"We haven't gotten that far yet. To determine who lives or dies." Gary assured him. "Right now we have to consider a lot of things, including the type of man you are." He paused. "So tell me, Dennis...what kind of man are you?"

Dennis stared at him. Wide eyed and confused. "I...I'm a father. Who wanted to do better for my child but then my wife, his mother, was murdered. I made some bad decisions a little before that, that landed me in prison and I just couldn't...I couldn't catch up and get my money right."

Gary nodded. "I hear you. For now I want you to get some rest and we'll talk about the next steps tomorrow." He looked at the taller man. "Untie him."

When Dennis' tied hand was unbound, he rubbed his throbbing wrist.

"Come with me," Gary said to Dennis.

"Where we going?"

Gary glared. "Don't you realize by now that we don't like questions?"

Dennis nodded.

Twenty minutes later Dennis was inside a large luxurious room with a huge cream king size canopy bed in the middle of the floor. A gigantic TV sat in front of it and it smelled of a woman. Flowery and sweet.

Seeing no available chair, Dennis carefully sat on the side of the bed and rubbed his painful leg, which had been shot some weeks back. Seconds later a beautiful thirty-three year old woman waltzed inside. Her skin was the color of un-cracked almonds and she had long silky hair running down her back. African American, her eyes were intense and large and there was a darkness, an evil behind them that couldn't be denied.

Wearing a red negligee, she seductively walked up to him and smiled. Instead of feeling relieved, her

By T. STYLES

jester sent chills down his spine. He knew in that moment that he was meeting *The Connect*.

"Comfortable?" She asked, running her fingertips along side his yellow face.

He nodded. "I...yes...I...uh..."

"Relax. I'm Nidia." She extended her hand. "And you are?"

He shook it softly and then kissed the top and bottom, not knowing what move was right but being too afraid to leave anything out. "Nervous." He swallowed the lump in his throat. "I'm nervous."

She sat next to him. "I would say you shouldn't be, but you know the severity of what you've done." Her brows lowered. "To me and my partners." She sat next to him. "Needless to say you've put us in quite a bind."

He nodded. "I know, and I'm sorry."

"Apologies don't stop my financial burden. You know that right?"

"Yes, and I'm gonna...I'm gonna do all I can to make you whole."

She smiled brighter. And Dennis could sense it was genuine but he wasn't sure why. What had he said in that moment that caused her to be so excited?

"Good, but there is no need to talk about money right now." She placed a heavy hand on his thigh and then ran her fingertips over his crotch. Her touch felt like a man although he could see she was all woman. "What I want you to do is get up and go take a shower." She pointed at a closed door. "When you're done, return here. To me."

Without the use of his cane, Dennis limped heavily into the bathroom and did as he was told. There was a window but it was high up so there was no escape. The space was burgundy and cream, with gold faucets throughout. It was as grand as the bedroom but he wasn't surprised. After showering, he was shocked to see when he opened the glass door, that fresh black silk boxers were sitting on the toilet seat.

He hadn't even heard anyone come inside.

You slipping, Dennis. He thought to himself.

After drying off and sliding into the boxers, he limped back into the bedroom. Only to be surprised to see Nidia, naked, sitting on her ankles. She looked like a work of art and still he trembled.

What did this sexy vixen want?

"Come here," she said extending her fingers toward him.

He slowly crawled into bed, lying face up. He was as stiff as a mannequin and had it not been for the thump of his heart she would've assumed he was dead.

Still, she straddled him and rubbed her fingers over his boxers. He was growing like fresh baked bread. "I see they fit. I can always guess a man's size."

He nodded. "Thank...thank you."

She outlined his slender chest muscles with her index finger. "Okay, here's where we are." She eased up, dipped into his boxers and removed his penis. He was already rock hard as she inserted him inside her body. "Like you already know," she moaned lowering her waist. "You have killed someone very important to me."

"Yes...yes...I...I'm sorry."

"Silence," she said softly.

He didn't know whether to enjoy himself or fuck the shit out of her like his body wanted. At the same time, if this was his last sex session, he wanted to go out with a bang. No pun intended.

"You're not sorry." She rode him slowly while moaning. "And that's okay." She placed both of her palms on the flat of his chest and rose and fell into him harder. "But...something just may work out for you after all." She ran her tongue over her top and bottom lip while she enjoyed herself quite a bit.

He nodded, trying his best not to bust inside of her.

"I'll do any...anything you say."

She fell on top of his body, her warm breasts smashing against his chest. "You should know...that I was going to kill him myself." Her hands snaked under the pillow behind his head and she rose slowly, bringing a knife with her.

"What the fuck?" He said eyeing the weapon.

Placing it at his neck, his eyes widened as he thought about fighting her in that moment. But fear and the feeling of ecstasy were messing with his head. Tossing his thoughts all over the place. But one thing did change. If she was going to kill him he was going to bust inside of her, so he began to pump harder. With a hand on each side of her waist like she belonged to him.

She kept the knife where it was and sliced softly into his flesh as they fucked.

He may have winced a little but his stroke never ceased. In that moment he was about his business.

"He owed money for over two months." She sliced him a little again. "And as a result, he started giving out my product without weighing the risks which put him more into debt. I think it was out of spite because he knew we were coming." She cut him lightly again, just enough to draw a little blood. "I was going to kill him. And then after learning that you took his life, I was going to murder you instead." She pumped harder. "But you don't die easily...even took to moving out here, to be near me. That makes you smart."

She smiled.

"Yes...I..."

"Shh...there's no need to talk. Because now, Dennis, you are going to pay back his debt. In full."

By T. STYLES

When he realized he wasn't going to die, but get cut a little by little instead, he felt somewhat relieved despite the small slashes littering his neck and face.

"Whatever you want," he moaned. "Whatever you want."

"That's what I love to hear." She bucked her hips wider and slammed into him so hard his body quivered as her ass moved up and down like thick waves. "I fucking...I fucking love to hear that." She continued to fuck like she hadn't a day in her life. "I'm cumming...I'm...I'm cumming." After being satisfied, she slammed on top of him out of breath. Back to business, she looked down at him. "You have two weeks."

He was about to bust too when she slid off of him and walked to the bathroom, leaving him with a dripping stiff dick that pointed upward.

He was about to jerk himself off when suddenly the door opened and the white man and Gary walked inside, grabbing him under his pits, and yanking him out of the room.

CHAPTER TEN

When the water was warm and sudsy enough, Banks turned off the faucet. He had placed candles around the bathroom and rose peddles throughout, hoping to make his girl smile. Lately she spent most of her nights crying and days avoiding him and he wanted some relief. He wanted them to be as they were in the past but at the very least he wanted them to be friends.

Even if she was mad.

Sitting on the edge of the tub he took a deep breath. "Nikki!" He yelled. "Come here!"

It took some time but eventually she appeared in the doorway. Her hair up in a ponytail, she was wearing one of his long t-shirts with nothing else underneath, since her clothing was at home.

Crossing her arms over her body she said, "What, Banks?"

"I ran a bath for you." He smiled. "Come get inside." He nodded toward the water. "I'll wash your back."

She looked at it, shook her head and walked away.

"Nikki...please."

Banks sat alone, crushed.

In the five days since his father had gone missing he had done all he could to make things right for Nikki and nothing worked. He even wondered if being alone, without her, would be better than having her with him in the house. But every time he nurtured that thought he pushed it out of his mind because simply seeing her face, even if she was sad, in a way made his day. His father was right after all.

But he wasn't going to give up yet.

After using some of the money Dennis left behind, the following day he made her favorite meal...baked spaghetti and meatballs. He figured since it had been days since she'd eaten she wouldn't be able to deny such a delicious meal. But Nikki's depression was genuine and like she did everything else, she turned away from the food, and she turned away from him.

After days of trying to make her feel better, he came to a realization. He wasn't going to let her suffer any longer. Not on his watch. So while they were seated on the sofa, watching TV, Banks looked over at her. "Nikki..."

Silence.

"Nikki." He cut the television off with the large remote. Now he had her attention. "Nikki, look at me." He paused. "Please." She looked up at him. "I'm gonna get you home."

"I said I don't want you to do that." She sighed and laid in a fetal position on the sofa. "Just leave me alone, Banks and cut back on the TV."

"I know you don't want me to do that," He sighed. "But I... I never wanted you here like this." He paused. "I never wanted you to hate me."

"I don't hate you." She sighed deeply.

"You hate my father." He paused. "And I don't want my name associated like that in anyway when it comes to you. So I'm gonna get you home. And I don't care what I gotta do to make it happen. I'll buy you a bus ticket."

She sat up and faced him. "But he'll get mad."

"Let me handle my father." He put his hand on her thigh. "Just give me some time."

"But your dad didn't leave us enough money, Banks."

"I know." He nodded and walked away.

The rain came down heavily on his head.

Banks started to postpone his plan but he had put it off for so many days that it was time to push off. Or else he would risk not being a man of his word, an act he couldn't afford if he wanted Nikki to ever forgive him.

Waiting for his prey, Banks hid in the corner of a dark building watching like a lion. He was dressed in a

By T. STYLES

black hoody and black sweatpants. His mind filled with larcenous thoughts, he was waiting for the perfect moment, to rob a lone dealer who was slinging a few feet up from where he stood. Banks had been watching him for almost an hour, so he could stack up as much cash as the drug dealer could stuff in his pockets. After the dealer served his last customer, Banks felt it was the perfect time to act.

So he rushed up behind him and pointed a stiff finger in his back. "I'm not..." he cleared his throat when his voice cracked. "I'm not fucking around...give me the money or I'll blow your back out!"

The Dealer kept his hands raised in the air. "Come on, man." He turned his head a little, but not enough to see Banks' young face. "Don't do this shit."

"You think I'm playing?" Banks asked through clenched teeth. "You think this a game?"

"Nah, but I gotta pay my rent and—"

"I don't give a fuck what you gotta pay!" Banks poked him harder in the spine.

"Aight, aight," he said. "Calm down." His hands rose higher.

"You got five—"

Before Banks could complete his sentence the dealer came down on his face with something long and silver. Immediately Banks felt a cool sensation on his cheek that instantly grew warm. When he touched the wet place and looked at his fingertips, he saw blood on his skin that washed away seconds later in the rain. The dealer had slashed the same location of his bullet wound, causing an X to appear on his face.

Banks fell down in shock and the dealer took off running.

Leaving Banks alone.

Standing in a filthy bathroom of a gas station, Banks stuck mounds and mounds of tissue on his face to stop the bleeding. Looking at himself through the grungy mirror, he couldn't believe his life had come to this. Broker than when he started, he was miserable. Not only had he failed, he was starting to hate the world and everybody in it.

He would murder a nigga just because, *if* he had a gun.

Looking down at his blood in the bathroom sink, he turned on the water to wash it away. Without turning it off, he walked out and made an attempt to find a way home.

Two hours later, a bloody mess, he trudged into the house. His shoulders were hunched over in defeat. But the moment Nikki saw him she ran toward him and hugged him multiple times. "Oh my God, Banks! I was so worried about you!" She separated from him. "And what happened to your face?" She touched the hardened blood soaked tissue sticking to the dried wound.

He walked around her. "I'm fine. I couldn't get the...I couldn't get the money."

He was about to walk to his room, when from the back, came three men he'd never seen before. They were Chris 38, Pete 19 and Brown 25 and all moved through the house as if they owned the place.

Banks looked at Nikki and back at them. "Who are they?" He asked her.

Chris laughed. "You can ask us, youngin," he said scratching his scruffy beard. "We got ears."

Banks frowned. "Who are you then?"

"I'm Chris and this my son Pete." He pointed to a kid who looked like him with his dark skin and scraggly beard that was making its way to the world. "This right here is Brown and he's my cousin." He pointed to a shorter man who was wearing thick-rimmed glasses. "I'm your father's brother."

Banks frowned again. He heard of them in the past, a little, but never saw their faces until now. "I thought my dad said ya'll were in prison."

They all laughed. "We were, but they let us out," Chris said. "They do that sometimes you know?" He chuckled harder. "Now we here."

Banks shuffled in place. "Why though?"

"Your father called and told us to meet him here. That's all I can say right now." He took a deep breath and moved closer to Banks. "And now tell me what happened to you."

"I'm sick of all this new shit," he said pushing past them and storming to the back of the house. "I'm sick of everybody."

Nikki followed.

By T. STYLES

CHAPTER ELEVEN

The Louisville's (Mason, Cruz, Kevin and Theo) were sitting in the living room waiting for Linden to return. About an hour ago he called and said he had some major information and they were on edge wondering what was so important. When the door opened and he finally arrived, everybody rose.

"What the fuck going on?" Kevin asked. "And what's so important you couldn't tell us on the phone?"

Linden locked the door. "Sit down, nigga." He trudged into the living room and pulled up a chair, placing it in front of them. "I'm 'bout to tell you."

Everyone took a seat.

Linden sat too. "I put the word out that I wanted to meet Pop's connect."

"And what happened?" Kevin asked.

"She ain't fucking with us," Linden said. "Her people said we were too reckless. They must've heard about us in New York and don't want the heat their way."

Everyone but Mason sighed.

"I thought you said they took your meeting." Cruz said as he scratched his dick. The last chick he fucked gave him crabs, which he had yet to cure.

Linden frowned. "I did go meet with one of them."

"So what was said?" Theo asked as he bit into chips.

"Pops owed money," Linden said with a deep breath. "A lot."

"Is it something we could make back?" Cruz asked, scratching harder.

"Can you stop rubbing your dick while you talking to me?" Linden snapped. "Ain't nobody trying to see that shit."

"But my balls itch."

"I don't give a..." Linden took a deep breath. The conversation with his sibling was goofy and distracting. "Pops was already into her for over a hundred large. Plus the pack he had when he died. The nigga Gary told me we gotta pay off that debt just to be able to breathe on the streets."

Kevin glared. "You mean that nigga died and left us in debt?"

Linden shrugged. "We can try and ditch 'em and not pay shit." He paused. "But if we do, we gonna be running for the rest of our lives."

"Fuck!" Kevin said slamming his fist into his other hand. "I should've never came up here!"

"You the one who wanted to drop everything and bounce!" Theo reminded him. "So don't act like—"

"I thought we would be getting paid!" He snapped. "Ain't nobody come out here for this mess."

"Well we ain't getting nothing but broker right now!" Cruz said, scratching again. "Man...I'm heated." He smelled his fingertips.

"Did they say who they dealing with now?" Mason asked quietly. "Somebody gotta supply Baltimore. Don't seem smart to leave the market hungry."

Linden grinned at Mason. "Ya'll dumb ass niggas asking the wrong questions and here lil' Mason go, getting down to the heart of the matter."

Kevin rolled his eyes.

"Well what she say then?" Theo asked.

"Dennis is alive," he said. "And they dealing with him now."

They threw their bodies back into their seats; a few ran their hands down their faces in frustration.

"You playing right?" Kevin said.

"Nah," Linden continued. "You know me better than that."

"Did you find out who killed dad?" Mason asked with a cracked voice. "I mean, is he, is he...gone?"

Linden took a deep breath. "He's dead. They not saying where the body is though. Or if they were involved but I know Dennis did it."

"So basically everything we thought was right," Kevin said. "Dennis killed pops and took the connect."

"Pretty much." Linden agreed.

Mason's temples throbbed. Not only was he hurt by what he was hearing, to learn that his father was never coming home again, but he also felt too young to be dealing with all of this alone. And yet he had no choice.

"I'm gonna kill him," Mason said under his breath.

"Kill who?" Linden smiled; happy the young buck was coming around, finally seeing things his way.

"Everybody," Mason promised. "Starting with Dennis."

CHAPTER TWELVE

A few days passed and Dennis was back home and making a living of running back and forth to Baltimore, supplying the connections he had made on his own and through Nidia, with the best cocaine. Since most of the trips were exhausting and stressful, because he never knew if the DEA was watching, he realized it was time to tap into the market right where he was so he wouldn't have to go so far.

In Houston, Texas.

After being up all night, Dennis pushed piles of dime bags to the right of the table. He, Chris, Pete, Brown and Banks spent all day and night bagging cocaine, and now, using his family's help, and their knowledge on the streets in Houston, it was time to get paid.

Nidia had explained that if Dennis met the deadline by paying off Arlyn's debt, that she would make him one of the richest men in the world, and in a short amount of time it was starting to look like his wealth would exceed even his own expectations.

She didn't tell him she was also getting money from the Lou's. That was her business.

After helping package, and talking to his father about Nikki, Banks wobbled to his room. All he wanted was to grab a quick nap but there was no time. He had to get dressed because he was going with Brown to make a drop, something he normally didn't do. But because the deadline was looming, they had to move quickly and that meant all hands on deck.

While sitting on the bed Nikki walked inside and hung in the doorway. "Are you okay?" She asked softly.

He nodded yes.

"Can I do anything?"

"Why you still here, Nik?" Banks asked. "When you first came all you wanted was to go home. I talked to Pops already. You free to do whatever. He won't stop you. I won't either."

She walked inside the room and sat next to him. "What you talking about?"

"I just told you." He shrugged. "Pops said you could bounce so why you still here?"

She sighed. "I don't want to...I mean...I'm worried."

"Don't be." He paused. "I'm good." He stood up and slipped on his hoody. It brushed over the X shape scar over his face and stung a little.

"You dealing drugs now, Banks? This ain't like you."

"And?" He shrugged. "I gotta do what I gotta do don't I? Why you worried about it anyway? Huh?"

She looked down. "Listen, Banks, I'm sorry about how I treated you. When your father first took me away from my cousin...I guess I...I mean, I didn't know you weren't involved."

"Why would I take you away from Elena? Don't you know me better than that?"

"I get that now." She paused. "But please don't be mad at me. Don't treat me like this."

"I'm not mad, just got a lot of stuff on my mind that's all." He paused. "And it's starting to make me not care about nothing no more."

"I hope you don't feel that way about me."

Silence.

"Is there anything I can do to help you?" She continued.

"No." He stood up and moved toward the door. Before walking out he turned around and looked at her. Taking a deep breath he said, "When I come back I don't want you here. Go home."

"Banks!" She yelled as he walked out. "Banks don't do this!"

The road was mostly empty as they cruised down the desolate street on the way to their destination. Banks preferred to be quiet, but it was obvious that Brown was a talker and this irritated Banks to no end.

"It's not that," Banks said. "I'm just different I guess."

Brown nodded as he drove down the street. "So different you can't tell your family how?"

Banks laughed. "I don't wanna be in any of this drug shit." He shrugged. "All I wanna be is somewhere I like, get a job that pays and live my life. Everybody I know who deals in coke dies."

"But what if you meant to have more?"

Banks laughed. "You mean by moving drugs?"

"Why not?"

Banks shook his head. "I don't got a good feeling about none of this." He shrugged. "But nobody listens to me. Like...like everybody keep saying...I'm a kid and I don't know how money can do good things in my life. But that ain't what I'm seeing."

Brown parked the car. "You ever heard of Baldwin IV of Jerusalem?"

Banks laughed.

"I'm serious," Brown continued. "You heard of him or not?"

Banks shook his head no.

"Well he was a king at the age of 13 and had leprosy too."

Banks frowned. "What's that?"

"A nasty disease that causes lesions." He grabbed the cocaine in a duffle out the back and they both exited the car. "Anyway at 13 he fought his first war and was successful." He paused. "You know how he did that?"

By T. STYLES

Banks walked alongside him on the dark street. "I just said I didn't know who he was."

"He did it because he had the tools necessary to rule." He pointed at him. "His daddy did that for him. Put that in his mind early on." Brown knocked at his own temple a few times. "And he started to believe it too. Convinced people around him of the same."

They walked up to a door and kicked on it softly. It was an old brick house with shattered windows and thick bunches of shrubs. Alongside them were massive piles of weeds growing out the ground. It definitely didn't look conducive for business.

"So you think something gonna happen to my Pops? Where I gotta do this shit on my own?"

Brown shrugged. "Anything can happen." He kicked harder. "You just better stay ready."

"Nah...it won't happen to us."

"Let's hope that—"

Suddenly a dark figure walked from the back of the house.

Banks spotted him immediately but was stunned silent and couldn't alert Brown in time. The white's of the man's eyes was all he could see on the robber's hooded face within the darkness. Within seconds the figure raised his gun and shot Brown in the back causing his body to fall forward, onto Banks, knocking them both to the ground.

Within seconds, the figure snatched the pack from Brown's hand and dipped past Banks. Blood from Brown's body sprayed on Bank's scarred face, causing his vision to be temporarily blurred.

Wiping his eyes, and thinking on his feet, Banks grabbed the gun Brown had on his hip and stood up. Taking off behind the figure. Realizing he was being chased, the man turned around and shot in his direction six times. Missing his shoulder by inches. But Banks was relentless and ran faster until he was so close he could touch his back.

His blood pumped hard and Banks' entire body trembled as he aimed the shaky weapon in the man's direction and squeezed the trigger.

BOOM!

By T. STYLES

CHAPTER THIRTEEN

Time passed and the Louisville's were miserable.

Money had dried up long ago and they resorted to stepping on cocaine so much that they were known as the *Tap Shoe Boys* on the street. Crack heads didn't buy from them unless the streets were dry. Being barely able to eat, or doing the simple things they wanted, started taking a toll on everything. They would've gone back to New York except they had burned many bridges and Nidia was expecting them to do just that. So she could put a bullet in each of their skulls for her troubles.

Instead of running, they all stayed in the two-bedroom apartment and got on each other's nerves so much it was hard to keep peace. From farting, to simply being in the way, they were about to kill each other if something didn't change soon. Luckily by robbing a few dope boys and selling garbage coke, they were able to make a dent in what they owed Nidia but they had a long way to go.

On edge, a cool breeze rolled over Mason and his brothers as they stood outside of the apartment building waiting on Linden. He told them to pack a light bag because they were taking a road trip. And when Linden finally pulled up in a brown 1988 Plymouth Grand Voyager, they piled inside.

Curious, Mason sat in the backseat while Cruz sat in the passenger's seat and Kevin and Theo in the middle row seats. Once they were settled, everyone realized the vehicle smelled new.

When all of the doors were closed Linden pulled off.

"Thought we didn't have no money," Mason said looking around, his hands peddling over everything.

Linden looked at him through the rearview mirror. "I borrowed it."

Kevin smirked knowing exactly what his brother meant.

"You gonna tell us where we headed now?" Cruz asked. "I was just about to fuck this sweet—"

"I'm not trying to hear that shit." Linden said cutting him off with a palm to the center of his face. His brother's horniness was enough to make him want to vomit at times. "This trip is about business."

"Then tell us more," Kevin said.

"I got an address." Linden said with a smile.

Kevin, Cruz and Theo all widened their eyes.

"Wait, you talking about—"

"Dennis." Linden said cutting Kevin off. "I finally know where he's laying his head and we in route now."

By T. STYLES

CHAPTER FOURTEEN

The sun was out and the birds chirped as Banks lie on his back looking at the wall in the house. Nikki had been inside his room earlier to open the window, to allow the winter's air to cool the space, but Banks didn't seem to appreciate any of her good gestures. His mind was some place else.

On the man he killed to save the pack even though Brown died.

Worried about his spawn, Dennis walked inside the room and sat next to him. "Did I tell you how I met your mother?"

Banks rolled over and looked at him.

Dennis sighed. "I loved her from the first time I saw her face." He smiled. "That smile of hers always made me weak. Them deer eyes and..." He sighed deeper. "She was everything, Banks." He stared at him harder. "But she was also married."

"I didn't know that."

"It's the truth." He sighed. "In fact, when we finally got married it wasn't even legal."

"Then how...I mean..."

"You can get away with anything if nobody cares who you are." He paused. "Trust me. And it wasn't like we had a bunch of money to cause the IRS or anybody else to be interested in our bigamy. We were just two people in love and living together illegally."

Banks sat up. "Where you going with this pops?"

"It's coming." He stood up and walked across the room. "Before we decided to be together she had this husband, like I said. Peteery Thompson was his name." He paused. "He used to sell moonshine out the back of his house. Made a lot of money doing it too. Had a lot of nice things. And one of the things he thought he owned was your mother, except he didn't. She belonged to me."

Knowing his father's dark side, and how easily he killed, Banks was certain that there was more. "What you do to him?"

"She called me one night. We had been dating but nothing official." Dennis wiped his hand down his face. "But what she said...on the phone...to this day it fucks up my mind."

"What was it?"

"Said he kept waking her up and choking her in the middle of the night. Said he had a feeling she wasn't in love with him anymore. And that he would kill her before he saw her with anybody else."

Banks scratched his head. The thought of his mother suffering caused him extreme agitation. "So how did she get the phone? To call you? And why didn't she—"

"Call the police?" Dennis said completing his sentence. "Because he would've killed her and they wouldn't care. A black man with a poor white woman."

He sighed. "Trust me it wasn't good. For anybody. So I was her hero." He paused. "It was 1:58 am when I crawled through the window with one of my neckties. I came up behind him while he was on top of her, choking her again, just like she said. Later she told me he was fucking her and his dick was rock hard because it was the only way he could have sex." He pointed at Banks. "The only difference now was that the choking had gotten rougher and more frequent." Dennis' eyes gazed over as he motioned with his hands how tightly he strangled him. "When I was done squeezing the life out of his body, I pushed him off of her and we got out of there. Together. Never looking back. And later having you."

"Why would you tell me something like that?" Banks scratched his short curly hair. "I'm not understanding."

"Because you killed a man, son." He paused. "And unfortunately you'll kill another. As you can tell by the niggas I dropped. You just have to make the bodies count. You just have to make sure it's worth it."

Banks jumped up. "I don't wanna kill somebody else! I want to—"

"What?" Dennis yelled. "Go back to a building full of niggas who want you dead? In Baltimore? Now I done told you that ain't your life no more! Move the fuck on!"

Banks looked at him intensely...his body trembling with rage. "I didn't want this."

"Stop saying that!" Dennis stabbed his hand into his fist. "Otherwise Brown would've died in vain. Is that what you saying?"

Nikki walked into the room.

They both looked back at her.

Dennis took a deep breath. "I'ma leave you with your girl." He pointed at Banks. "But I highly suggest you get used to one thing, this our new life." He walked out.

Nikki closed the door and pushed Banks into a seated position. She removed her pants and shirt and stood naked in front of him. Slowly she eased on his lap, her legs spread apart.

"What you doing, Nik?" He whispered.

"You gonna fake like you don't know no more?" She paused. "I know it's been months but—"

"I know what you doing I'm just asking why?" He paused. "Why you still here?"

"Come on, Banks...its time to make up." She kissed his lips. "Please."

Tired of fighting, Banks smiled and slowly eased his finger into her waiting body. She was warm and horny, just the way he liked it. In the mood, he continued to finger fuck her until she was so wet her juices oozed down his wrist.

"Still mad at me?" She asked.

By T. STYLES

"Never mad."

She kissed his lips. "Good...because I love you, Banks. And I don't wanna be anywhere else. But here."

"No matter what?"

"No matter what." She pushed him to the bed and removed his clothes before going down on him until he screamed her name.

The Louisville's looked at Dennis who was standing outside of his house with Pete and Chris, smoking cigarettes. They were so engrossed in conversation about losing Brown due to betrayal that they didn't see the van full of killers on the curb.

"What we gonna do?" Kevin asked, his .45 sitting in his lap, ready to fire.

"We kill them," Linden said.

Kevin quickly moved to open the door until Linden grabbed his wrist.

"At the right time. Something feels off." Linden paused. "But don't worry...we gonna do it soon."

Linden pulled up to the rundown motel and parked in an available space in front of their room. The car ride had been completely quiet after leaving Dennis's house, each wanting to say something but reserving their words to prevent blowing up. Or getting punched in the face by their oldest sibling.

Linden looked at his brothers. "I know ya'll mad."

"Nigga, we fucked up!" Kevin yelled. "We had them bang to rights and you let 'em go? Why would you drive us all the way down this bitch if we gonna let 'em breathe? I'm not understanding."

"Because something didn't feel right." He said. "And we have to be smart when we do it that's why. Don't worry, we not going home without completing the job."

"Smart or scared?" Cruz asked. "Which one?"

"You questioning me?" Linden pointed to himself. "I'm the one who found them remember?"

"Where Banks at?" Mason asked under his breath. "He there?"

"I didn't see him." Linden paused. "I'm sure he is though. Why?"

Mason shook his head. "Whatever we do, we gotta make sure we get him too."

"So finally you coming around?" Kevin said.

"That ain't it," Mason added.

"Then what is it?" Linden asked.

"The night I saw dad...the last time he was alive...I was in the car. And Banks was too."

Everyone looked at him.

"What you mean you were in the car?" Linden asked, nostrils flaring.

"Dennis dropped me off at the house and dad got in the car. Pops told me to get out but he didn't seem right. Like he was mad or something...and then—"

"He never came back," Linden said. "Must've been the night he killed him."

"Why you just telling us now though?" Kevin asked.

He shrugged. "I'm telling you now because I don't give a fuck about shit no more."

"You know what..." Cruz unlocked the door abruptly. "Fuck this little nigga. Fuck everybody!" He stormed out, slamming the door behind himself.

"I'm going with him," Theo said. "Where ya'll headed?"

"To get some chicken," Linden said, trying not to strangle the life out of Mason for keeping such a crazy secret for so long.

"Bring back some biscuits too. Don't eat 'em all in the car like last time." He exited the stolen ride.

"You staying?" Linden asked Kevin.

Kevin looked back at Mason and rolled his eyes before focusing on Linden. "Yeah, I'm rolling. Might as well. Ain't shit else to do."

Linden pulled off.

Cruz and Theo sat in the room watching TV drinking beer. They were still mad about not being able to hit the Wales Family but due or die; they were going to make their move the next day. Even if Linden didn't sanction the murders.

For the moment all was right with the world and they were laughing at reruns of *The Jeffersons* when suddenly the bathroom door flew open and two gunmen, wearing ski masks unloaded bullets into both of their bodies, before walking out the front door.

Blood splattered on the walls.

Little did they know, earlier, another car sat on the curb of the Wales' property watching all activity that came and exited the neighborhood. After Brown was killed, due to a set up, the Wales' figured one of their connections was foul so they needed the extra security. It didn't take long for a few calls to be made, which resulted in learning exactly who they were and where they were posted up.

And now the Lou's were a couple members short.

By T. STYLES

CHAPTER FIFTEEN
FCI LOW - DORM
PRESENT DAY - CHRISTMAS EVE

Tops looked around at the men who were all glued onto his every word as he told the story of how the vicious war between the Wales and The Lou's, which ripped through the streets of Baltimore and Texas, began.

"You gotta tell us which one he is," Byrd said looking down at the inmate on the floor. He was as excited as a child listening to Christmas stories on the Eve.

"Who said it's Mason or Banks?" Tops paused. "You see that's where people get shit wrong." He pointed at him. "They assume that the Lou's and Wales beef was only about them two niggas. But a lot of dudes died over this shit. And many more after they murdered the brothers in the motel too."

"I be back." Kirk said as he looked down at the inmate and then Tops.

The moment Kirk walked away, Tops glared at Byrd with a lowered brow. "Follow that nigga." He paused. "We don't want him alerting the C.O.'s." He looked down at #11578. "Besides, this nigga not gone yet."

"I'm on it." Byrd jumped up and caught Kirk just before he walked out the dorm. "Where you going, nigga?"

Kirk frowned. "To the bathroom." He crossed his arms. "Why? You wanna hold my dick or something?"

"Bathrooms that-a-way." Byrd pointed behind him with his thumb.

"Look, why you following me?" Kirk frowned. "I don't even know you like that."

"I'm following you because I asked a fuckin' question that I still ain't get an answer to."

"I'm not comfortable with what's going on back there," Kirk said. "What if he dies and they try to pin the shit on us?"

"Won't happen." Byrd shook his head.

"Why not?"

"Because we didn't stab the nigga that's why."

"That won't stop them from convicting—"

Suddenly Byrd placed a firm hand on his shoulder and squeezed lightly. "Come back to the room with me." He smiled. "We missing story time."

Kirk considered busting him in the center of the nose, so he could slurp his own blood. Instead he reluctantly walked back into the dorm with Byrd. The moment Tops saw Kirk he smiled. "Sit down, man. You about to miss the best part."

"I'm good," Kirk responded.

"Nigga, sit the fuck down!"

Slowly Kirk sat on the edge of someone's bunk.

Tops cleared his throat. "Like I said, the war took two major turns after Arlyn was killed. And the first started like this…"

CHAPTER SIXTEEN
1993 - FIVE YEARS LATER

Time had passed and shit had changed.

For the worst.

Nineteen-year-old Mason stood across the street from a boarded up brick house smoking a cigarette. He stared at the house intensely, before his eyes moved up and down the block. Wearing a black hoody and black sweatpants, he looked as if he was up to no good.

To be honest he was.

Tossing the cigarette on the ground, cautiously he crept toward the boarded up house, hopped over the lopsided fence and ran around back. Once there he looked around and when the coast was clear, he removed a wooden slat, crawled down the steps and covered the hole above his head again.

Using a key he walked inside where his brothers Linden and Kevin were seated in the dark living room loading weapons. This space was a disaster. Mold on the walls and in the air. A dark, damp brown carpet under their feet. The two-bedroom basement apartment was definitely no place for a human to be living let alone breathing. And yet the Lou's called it home.

Over the years, wrinkles had etched themselves into Linden's forehead and hair had grown out over his face. Kevin on the other hand had allowed himself to gain so much weight he wasn't comfortable doing anything, including sitting or taking a shit. At over three hundred pounds of fat and blood, he believed he would die at any moment.

His brothers agreed.

"How much you get?" Linden asked as he tucked his nine in the back of his pants and grabbed another gun to load.

Mason dipped into his pocket and removed six hundred dollars, give or take a few bucks. He dumped the cash on the table littered with carryout boxes and empty beer bottles.

"Damn, lil' nigga," Linden grinned looking up at him. "You stay bringing in that paper."

Mason crossed his arms over his chest. "I have too." He flopped on the sofa and removed his boots. "I gotta pull the weight for everybody in here."

"Fuck that's supposed to mean?" Linden growled.

"It means everything! I mean look at where we living."

"You know it's temporary." Kevin said scratching his belly, which had broken out with eczema so bad the rash, cracked and bled.

"You said that a year ago," Mason reminded him. "And we still in the same place doing the same shit. I'm sick of living like this."

"Then what you wanna do?" Linden said scratching his nappy beard causing a crackling sound. "Huh? Because wanting things to be different and making them different are not the same."

He looked at his brothers intensely. "I say we go at them harder."

Linden gazed at Kevin and they both broke out into heavy laughter. "You act like we haven't been trying to do that already!" Linden yelled. "They fucking killed Cruz and Theo."

"That was five fucking years ago!" Mason continued pointing at the door. "I thought after we paid off Nidia we would be up from under this beef."

"Maybe we would have if you hadn't killed five Wales men," Kevin said.

"What I'm saying is that unless we get the inner circle, and break them down, we gonna stay living like cockroaches and rats. While they down south getting money everywhere. Even in Bmore." He took a deep breath. "I'm not with it no more."

"You talking a lot of shit, Mason," Kevin said. "But I still haven't heard a plan."

"Just wait...but trust me, what I got in mind gonna change everything." Mason nodded and grinned sinisterly.

By T. STYLES

Mason pulled up in a stolen Mercedes Benz in front of a small cream house in a low crime area, right behind a 1992 silver Camry with paper tags. Once parked, he pulled a tag off the stolen Fubu sweatshirt he was wearing and looked down at himself, to be sure everything was in order. He also dusted the loose hairs off his forehead; courtesy of the haircut he received an hour earlier.

When the door opened and an attractive seventeen-year-old girl bounced out, he pulled up on her right before she got into her Camry.

Slowly he rolled his window down and looked at her through the passenger side. "Excuse me," he said with a smile. "Can I holla at you for a second?"

She stopped and peeked into the car.

"I don't bite," he continued.

She smiled and observed the shiny ride that made her cotton panties moist. But more than anything the teen liked what she saw. Mason's large eyes, wavy hair and winning smile had her sick, and yet he seemed familiar in a strange way. Like she knew him in another place and time although she didn't know how.

"What you wanna talk to me about?" She leaned in the passenger window.

"Come on, man," he said smiling. "You gonna make me beg?"

She looked down and hunched her shoulders. "Ah, ahn...I would never make you beg."

"Well do you gotta man?"

"Nope," she said proudly. "He broke up with me so he wouldn't have to take me to the prom." A sadness came over her.

"Then he dumb."

That quickly he took her pain away and she giggled.

"I'm serious," he continued. "Any dude who won't make you his full time is crazy." Just then *Sex Me* by R. Kelly came on the radio and he turned it up trying to trick the mood for his advantage.

"That's my song," she said pointing inside the car.

He unlocked the door. "Well get in so you can hear it better."

"But I gotta go to my friend's house. To study."

"Do you have to or do you want to?" Mason continued. "There's a difference."

She looked at him harder. "Where do I know you from?"

"People say I look like a lot of niggas." He paused. "But I'm just me." He winked. "So you gonna get in or not? We need to start now if we gonna spend the rest of our lives together."

She giggled again, gazed around and then back at her house. Taking a deep breath she grabbed the handle and slid inside the car. Sealing whatever would happen next in her life. "Where we going?"

"I'm gonna take you out to eat first." He pulled off before she could change her mind.

She nodded. "My cousin would be so mad if she knew I got in this car." She placed on her seatbelt.

"Why you say that?"

She shrugged. "She's extra protective. Always telling me don't trust people and stuff like that. But never telling me why."

"Sounds like your cousin got a hard life."

"Not really...I mean...I don't think so anyway. We used to be close but I haven't seen her in years. But I talk to her like everyday." She took a deep breath. "She even bought me my first car."

"Seems like she's solid." He pulled up at a light. "What's her name?"

"Nikki." She paused. "She getting married soon to her fiancé. At least she wants to." She sighed. "His name is Banks."

He turned his head away from her and glared. "Is that right?" He clenched his jaw.

She nodded.

"You know what...you should call her."

"And say what?" She giggled.

"That I'm your new nigga." He squeezed her cheek. "And that as of now you belong to me."

CHAPTER SEVENTEEN

Looking at his pager, Banks bopped through the front door of the mansion he owned with his family, where he lived for over three years. After having surgery a few weeks back, he was still sore when the doctor removed the stitches.

Banks' body was his temple and over time he had put on a little more weight, thereby getting rid of the slender physique he had become accustomed to as a child in exchange for the body of a man. But he was far from fat, instead he was the perfect height to weight ratio, causing him to look more masculine. In addition, hair had smoothed out over his face, giving him a fine goatee and mustache.

The glowing light from the overhead chandeliers touched the gold chain that lie against his black t-shirt, causing it to sparkle.

Banks Wales looked like money.

Because Banks Wales *was* money.

Boxes lined the walls of the house because the Wales Family made an important decision, to move back to the Baltimore area to rule. Besides, most of their clientele was there and they were losing cash in transport alone due to consistent robberies.

At the end of the day it was time to go home.

"Hey, Nik!" Banks said placing his keys on the table next to the door. "Where you at?" He was almost in the back when she came running and leaping into his arms. He caught her dead on, allowing each of her thick yellow legs to dangle alongside his body. "Hey you," he said kissing her softly.

"Do you know what today is?" Her smile was so wide it took up her entire lower face.

"Nah," he said biting his bottom lip.

She kissed him repeatedly over his cheeks, forehead and lips. "Stop playing!" She giggled.

He grinned. "For real, tell me what's today."

She slapped his arm. "Stop playing, Banks." She ran her finger over the X scar on his face as the diamond on her engagement ring sparkled.

"Why you asking me something crazy?" He smacked her thick ass and it jiggled in response. "You know I know what today is."

She wrapped her arms around his neck. "I knew it."

"Have I ever forgotten your birthday?" Still holding her, he pulled out a set of Benz keys. "Ever?" They dangled in front of her, the Mercedes emblem shining.

She hopped down and snatched them from him. "Are you, are you serious?"

He nodded toward the door. "Look out front."

Excited, she walked slowly toward the exit and pulled the knob. Covering her lips, she saw a brand new white Benz in their driveway. She looked back at him. "Banks, oh my God!" Tears begin to fill her eyes. "It's just how I wanted it."

"You deserve that and more."

She rushed up to him, kissed him again and ran barefoot to her car.

Watching the love scene, Dennis walked out the house using his cane and stood next to Banks. "Wow...you bought it for her."

Banks nodded. His attention on the love of his life. "Wait till she sees the house."

"I'm happy for you." Dennis sat in one of the chairs on the front porch. "She's a real one. Definitely deserves the spoilage." He took a deep breath. "Sit next to me, son. I wanna talk to you."

Banks looked back at him suspiciously but complied. "What now, Pops?" His sight was still on Nikki.

"The Lou's hit two of our men again last night."

Banks sat back and dragged his hands down his face. "Who?"

"Trey and Clark."

Banks leaped up and glared down at him. "When you find out?"

"Keep your voice down!" Dennis warned. "You don't want her getting scared and threatening to leave again."

"Trey and Clark got kids and wives," Banks said through clenched teeth.

"I know, son." He nodded. "That's what makes this worse."

"Trey was gonna be in my wedding and everything."

"I'm sorry about your ceremony, son. I really am."

Banks glared at him. "It's like we can't get a fucking break. I'm sick of the bloodshed and shit."

"I understand."

"Do you?" Banks snapped. "They hit three of ours, we hit four of theirs. It's like we in the murder business instead of the money business."

"Son, the Lou's don't have nothing left. We officially took out their whole team and now they on the run. It's just a matter of time before they done and won't have a choice but to leave the state. Hell, to leave the country."

Banks looked over at Nikki who was grinning in his direction through the inside of the car.

"I want out," Banks said as he winked at his girl, while placing a large smile on his face to put on that everything was good.

"You just bought Nikki a car and the house in Reisterstown she don't even know about." He paused. "You sure you wanna do this now?"

"I got money, dad." He paused. "Enough to set me and Nik up. And enough to help pay off the last pack from Nidia."

"You been saving that much?"

Silence.

"One of these days you'll realize that the coke business is your life. That coke is in your blood. I know because I put it there." Dennis stood up. "I just hope it's sooner than later. I'm tired of having this conversation with you. Me and you both know you ain't going nowhere." He paused. "The movers will be back soon. Be ready to leave."

Banks walked into his bedroom after being out all night moving the last of their coke in the streets of Houston. Removing a pill bottle from his pocket, he tossed a few in his mouth and flopped on the edge of the bed. The only furniture left in the house was a mattress in each room, which they weren't taking anyway.

"Nikki, where you at?" He yawned. "I don't feel like going out tonight. I'll take you somewhere tomorrow." When his pager beeped he removed it from his hip, glanced at the number and clipped it back. "Nikki!" He yawned. "Where you at?"

When she didn't answer he got up and walked through the empty house calling her name, his voice echoing loudly.

Banks was still yelling Nikki when Dennis walked in the front door and saw what looked like fear on Banks' face. "What is it?"

"You seen Nikki today?"

"No...why?"

"Well she...she ain't here."

Dennis smiled.

"Fuck so funny?" Banks asked.

"You just bought her a new car last night."

"And?"

Dennis laughed. "You really expect her to be home when she had her dream car in the driveway? I wouldn't be surprised if she drove back to Maryland to show her cousin. You know how she is about that kid. Ain't it been a few years since she saw her anyway?"

"Longer than that." Banks sighed and wiped his hand down his beard, stopping at his chin. "But Nikki wouldn't do that. She knows it's too dangerous without me." The car was gone but he didn't think she'd be dumb enough to take a ride to Baltimore.

Dennis threw his hand up while the other maintained control of the cane. "Guess we gotta stay here until she comes back."

"I can hang here by myself." Banks replied. "You can go make sure the movers set up your house in Maryland."

"Nope. I'm staying with you. Can't move in right now anyway." Dennis sighed. "Pete and Chris have a meeting with a few customers out here. So I have to wait on them."

"Do whatever you want," Banks said. "I just know I'm not going nowhere."

One day turned into three and before long it was evident that something was wrong. Nikki and Banks had their arguments before, resulting in her spending a half a day in expensive hotel rooms but she never stayed away all day. He was like her fuel, and she needed him for both her emotional and physical well-being.

After cruising the streets of Houston and sending men on the blocks of Maryland to find his bitch, mainly Baltimore, Banks was losing his mind. He and his family even put word on the street that he was willing to pay to get her back and it wasn't until that moment that he got some new information.

"I don't trust it, Banks," Dennis said as he watched him pack money into a grey duffle on his bed. "You should take somebody with you. Don't go out in the streets alone when you don't even know if they have her or not."

"They told me not to bring anybody." He zipped the bag closed and grabbed his gun, stuffing it behind his jeans. "I can't take a chance. I'll be alright."

"See this is when your age fucks you up." Dennis said pointing at him. "You can't do shit by yourself."

"I gotta do this, Pops." Banks grabbed the bag and walked past Dennis.

"You see, you my son and I'm not gonna be able to stay out of it." He paused. "Not this time." He sighed. "So Chris and Pete going with you. Don't try to talk me out of it. I already told them to go when they get back."

Two hours later Banks stood in front of an abandoned building in an office park. It was mostly dark except for the streetlight on the corner next to them. Every time somebody moved in the distance, Banks would walk in the direction of the figure, while holding over one hundred and fifty thousand dollars in cash in a duffle. Pete and Chris had to snatch him back several times to calm down.

But they didn't understand.

Nikki wasn't like one of the bitches they fucked to pass time. She was the first girlfriend who understood him and his needs. They spent hours talking about the future and how to build a family together when the time was right. She kept him strong and sane, in a world that over the past five years had gotten more than strange.

And that made her priceless.

"You gotta calm the fuck down, Banks," Chris said as Pete looked on and observed their surroundings. "You gonna fuck around and attract another killer who ain't got nothing to do with this shit."

"Another killer?" Banks said.

Chris shrugged, realizing he was already proclaiming his girl as dead. "You know what I mean." Chris sighed. "I ain't trying to be presumptuous but this shit don't feel right."

"Don't feel right to me either," Pete added.

After fifteen more minutes in the darkness, a black beat down car with tinted windows pulled up to the threesome. Everyone was on immediate alert, while Chris and Pete's hands hovered over the weapons on their hips. After what seemed like forever, the window slowly rolled down and two unknown men smiled at the trio.

"You know us, nigga?" Pete glared. "Cause if you don't you can get the fuck from 'round here."

"Nah." The driver said. "You don't know me."

"Then what you want?" Banks asked.

"Nothing." The passenger said before looking at the driver and back at the Wales family. "But, aye, what's in that bag right there?" He pointed at it.

Thinking it was all a game, Banks got heated. "Nigga, ain't nobody playing with your bitch ass! Bounce before we—"

POP! POP! POP!

Gunfire from behind put the Wales family on high alert.

Banks broke to the left and the car pulled off, leaving tire tracks on the ground, grey smoke in the air. Banks could hear another set of feet running behind him but he didn't bother to turn around to see who was on his trail. His life was in danger and he had to fly if he wanted to survive.

When he was far enough away from the scene, he looked behind him at Pete, his twenty-four-year old cousin. He was relieved. Out of breath, and in fear for their lives, they hid behind another building and looked in the direction they just exited.

"I...I think they got Chris," Pete said breathing heavily. "They shot my Pops!"

Banks flopped on the ground, knees in the air. "FUCKKKKKKK!"

By T. STYLES

CHAPTER EIGHTEEN

K evin and Linden sat in the living room inside the house they rented in Pikesville Maryland. Although the Lou's wanted to get back into the drug business, for now they were making a living as hired killers. The money was decent but not great and they had intentions on changing that by killing Dennis and hopefully getting back into Nidia's good graces.

When the news came on Kevin turned the television as they both were glued to the channel.

"Elena Howard was found dead behind a Baltimore County public high school this morning." The newscaster said. *"Authorities are asking for any information leading to the capture and arrest of the perpetrator."*

Kevin looked at Linden who shook his head.

"Police are also looking for Nikki Howard, her cousin, for questioning. If you have any information please contact the number below."

Kevin turned the TV off and tossed the remote on the floor. "This gonna come back on us." He paused. "We can't control the lil' nigga no more."

"So what you suggest?" Linden asked. "Put space between us? Move out and leave him alone?"

"You know I'm not saying that, Lin."

"Good. Because like it or not he still family."

"Who's off the hinges right now."

Linden sighed. "Mason has a dark side that we might not always agree with. I'll give you that much. But I think with age he'll be king. Plus he bringing money in and that's what we need right now." He paused. "While you can barely walk two blocks without losing your breath. If something kicks off you'll be the first to go."

Kevin glared. "King of what?" He yelled. "We ain't got shit."

"That's your problem. You think small." He paused. "If it ain't in front of you, you can't believe it. Can't see the vision. That's why you'll never have nothing."

Kevin sighed. "Whatever..."

"Mason never got over his friend's father being behind Pop's murder," Linden continued. "But with a little time we gonna be on top because whatever he puts his mind to, he does it with all seriousness. Even revenge."

"How you figure, man?"

"Mason got heart." Linden stood up and grabbed a large brown paper bag off the table. "And that's all we need to take our place in this fucked up ass city."

Linden walked to the back room, were Nikki was stretched out on the bed, her arms and legs were tied to the posts. She was drugged up and asleep and yet Mason sat in a chair across from the mattress, gazing at her as if they were talking.

Confused, Linden walked up to him and looked at her before focusing back on his brother. "How long you gonna wait?"

"Wait for what?" Mason grabbed a beer can off the floor and took a large gulp.

"The fellas said you had them go to the spot to meet Banks but told them not to take the money." He paused. "Is this a mental game? If it is you moving dumb because we could've used that cash."

"It's not about the money."

Linden sighed. "It never is with you and Banks. Why though? What is it about him that makes me sense you're still loyal to him?"

Mason rolled his eyes.

Linden sat on the foot of the bed and looked at Mason. "Did you know dad had a talent?"

"What, man?" Mason frowned. He was irritating at best because all he wanted was to be left alone.

"Pops...did you know he had a talent?"

Mason shrugged not caring either which way.

"He was a painter. A good one too." He pointed at him. "And it helped him get over his anger." He reached in the brown bag and pulled out paintbrushes and paint. Linden stood up and placed the items on the table near Mason. "The easel's in the car." Linden sat back down. "I think you should take up a hobby man, to let go of some of this rage."

Mason looked at the supplies and then past him at Nikki. "Do you think he loves her?"

Linden looked at Nikki. "Don't know. Why?"

"He does. And I'm gonna keep her from him until it kills him so much he bleeds. From the inside."

CHAPTER NINETEEN

Onyx's *'Slam'* banged from the speakers inside Dennis' new luxurious mansion. He held off on placing all of his furniture inside his new home because he wanted to celebrate moving back to Reisterstown, a suburb in Baltimore County. After paying off Nidia and continuing to move the cocaine he purchased from her, his life had grown to levels he never thought were attainable.

Money was at his complete disposal these days and he spared no expense for the evening. Dennis hired caterers, dancers and even a magician to make the night go down in history. Although the original purpose of the party was his success, he bumped up the glitz and glamour of the evening all to increase Banks' mood.

It didn't work.

At the end of the day Banks was in a different place mentally. And physically too. Standing in the backyard he was coming to the realization that maybe Nikki left him of her own free will after all.

"I'm not understanding you right now," Banks said as he talked to Nikki on a bulky cell phone. "This doesn't seem like you."

"What's not to understand?" She said softly. "My cousin died because of you, Banks. And I wanted to call you personally to say it's over."

He took a deep breath. "Well how come you don't sound like yourself? Like you high or drunk?"

"I needed to do something to make myself feel better." She sighed. "Just leave me alone." She said a little louder. "Don't come looking for me anymore. Do you hear what I'm saying? I'm done with you."

Something didn't feel right to him.

"Nikki, if somebody is holding you against your will and you need my help, say these words...*I'll hate you forever.*"

Silence.

"Nikki...say it." He paused. "And trust me I'll tear up Houston looking for you."

She sobbed harder. "You're so far off its not even funny," she cried. "Just let me go."

CLICK.

"Nikki!" He yelled into the phone. "Nikki!"

After looking down at the screen and seeing the call had ended, he tossed it across the yard in a rage. This was rough. Losing Nikki was the worse pain he ever endured, second only to the day he saw his mother get murdered before his young eyes. After that bout of rejection, he was starting to nourish hate in the pit of his stomach and he wanted the world to know.

With hunched over shoulders, slowly he trudged back into the house and was inundated with loud music that caused him an extreme migraine. He thought about getting a room since his house was empty and he hadn't furnished it. Seeing the sadness on his son's face, Dennis rushed across the room with a glass of Moet in hand.

He handed the flute to him as he led him past the many people crowding the space. Off the living room of the elaborate home was a smaller room where they were somewhat alone. Just one other person was present who was asleep on top of a stack of purses and jackets.

Banks sat the flute on the floor, shoved the items aside and plopped down, his elbows on his knees. Hands clutched tightly together.

Dennis sat next to him. On someone's MCM purse.

"What is it, son?"

"I'm done, Pops." Banks shook his head. "I'm done."

Dennis smiled. "She finally convinced you it's over?"

"Even if she didn't...even if I didn't hear her say the...say it was over, I'm realizing I can't have no girl out here. It's too much...it's..." He took a deep breath. "I'm in, Pops. I'm talking all the way."

Dennis' eyes lit up. "Are you saying what I think you are?"

"From here on out my focus is on money." He pointed at the floor. "Fuck everything else."

Dennis grinned. A part of him felt bad seeing as how he came by getting his son's full attention on the family business. Due to losing Nikki. But on the other hand it was like music to his ears. With his son at his side he could take over the coke world. "That's what I like to hear." Dennis stood up with the help of his cane. "Wait right here."

Five seconds later he returned with a cute brown skin girl with a wide smile and a phat ass. Her name was Peaches and she smelled just like the fruit.

Banks immediately got uncomfortable and readjusted himself in his seat. This was the last thing he wanted and it was just another example of how disconnected Dennis was to his needs. "Pops, you know I'm not—"

"Just enjoy yourself."

Peaches extended her hand. "You coming with me, Mr. Wales? I promise I'll make it worth your while."

An hour later the party had grown thicker than African hair.

And Dennis stood in the middle of it all with a smile on his face. Five years back he couldn't afford to feed his son and now he was feeding a room full of people lobster, crab and shrimp. With bottles of Champagne that flowed like water to wash it down.

At the end of the day he was on top of the world.

When *Lately* by Jodeci blasted from the speakers, and the lights dimmed, a cute young girl started dancing on Dennis' lap. Enjoying the attention, Dennis could feel himself rising and he thought about taking her upstairs and grabbing a quick wet treat. But he wanted to make sure Banks was okay before disappearing and he got his answer when Peaches came from upstairs with an angry look on her face.

She moved quickly toward Dennis.

On high alert, he pushed the young girl off of him and hobbled up to her. "What's wrong?"

Peaches's wild eyes steered around. "That's gonna cost you extra." She extended her hand.

"Whatever, bitch." Dennis flagged a few of his men over with his cane. "Get this hoe out my house." They escorted her out the party with her screaming obscenities all the way. He watched from the large window in his foyer, the woman being thrown into a car and driven off the property.

A few minutes later Banks came from upstairs and curious, Pete walked up to him. "What happened to her?" Pete hadn't been right since Chris had been killed and so he took to the bottle more than usual. But after seeing Peaches' face, even he sobered up a little.

"I don't wanna talk about it." Banks said.

"You sure, man?" Pete continued. "Because she seemed irritated."

Dennis saw the two conversing and approached the duo. Still mad, Banks looked at his father and stormed off.

"Is somebody gonna tell me what the fuck happened?" Pete asked Dennis.

"Come walk with me." Dennis said, wanting to move away from the party and the slow music that caused everyone to be on full hump and grind mode on the dance floor.

The two walked outside, in the front yard where the massive driveway was littered with parked cars.

"When we go back inside, I want you to shut it down," Dennis told him.

"The party?" Pete asked.

"What else?"

"But Nidia coming later." Pete responded. "Said she had something for you remember?"

Dennis grinned. "Got it already."

Pete's eyes widened. "It wasn't sex was it?"

"That woman is insatiable." He laughed. "Even with age she just...she's something else." He pointed at him. "Hornier than a room full of fourteen-year-old boys in a strip club. But I like it."

"Why is she like that though?" Pete shrugged. "She too pretty to be so fucking horny."

Dennis shrugged. "Never found out the full reason. But they say her ninth grade teacher kidnapped her when she was young. Was passed around to his friends for five years before they finally found her all beaten and crazy. When they did get her back her father didn't want her anymore. Too much shame around her." He paused. "So the streets got to her instead and before long she met and married a Columbian who introduced her to coke." He sighed. "When he died, or was murdered, she kept the business alive."

Pete nodded having understood the mysterious Nidia for once. "So what's going on with Banks and that girl?"

Dennis looked behind him and saw Banks walking out the mansion.

"Go get me some cigarettes," Dennis told Pete. "I wanna talk to him alone."

"Okay."

"Wait!" Banks yelled rushing up behind them. "If you 'bout to go to the store I'm rolling with you." He paused. "I need to get out this house."

"Nah," Dennis said. "You staying with me."

Banks rolled his eyes. "One of these days you gonna realize I ain't a kid."

"Go without him," Dennis told Pete, ignoring Banks altogether.

Pete nodded and looked at the cluttered driveway. "But my car blocked."

Dennis dug into his pocket and tossed him his BMW keys. "Take mine."

"Bet." Pete winked and walked away.

"Why you ain't want me to go with him?"

"Nidia doubled our package."

Banks looked back toward the house where he saw many people slow dancing through the open window but no Nidia and her entourage in sight. "Again?"

"Ain't no need in looking...she gone already," Dennis said. "And if you ever meet with her never go to her room. She a freak."

"You ain't never gotta worry about that with me." Banks sighed, being tired of sex altogether. "But you think we can handle more weight?"

"Look at our lives, son. We doing it already."

Banks nodded. "Then I guess we gonna be—"

BOOM!

A massive orange cloud exploded from Dennis's car causing the front of the mansion to glow a fiery yellow. The windows shattered, sending thin pieces of glass into the flesh of all those near like biting mosquitoes. Afraid for his son, Dennis knocked Banks to the ground, his body covering his.

From up under his father, Banks looked toward the BMW, knowing Pete was gone and screamed. "NOOOOOOOOOOOOO!"

CHAPTER TWENTY

The fall air rolled through Pikesville Maryland smooth as fuck.

It was the perfect temperature to hang out and enjoy both the warm and cool weather and the Lou's were taking full advantage.

Mason, Kevin and Linden stood outside of their house celebrating taking down yet another general in the Wales' clan. Cars of the partygoers lined the block as neighbors came over periodically to throw a monkey wrench into the event, complaining of not being able to park in front of their own homes.

But it was a celebration!

Linden was bopping his head to the music as he stood in front of his grill, tossing hamburgers over the fire. When he saw the serious look on Mason's face, he put down his spatula and walked over to him.

Mason sat down.

Taking a deep breath, Linden grabbed a beer from the cooler and flopped in the chair next to him. "Why you over here looking crazy?"

"It ain't over." Mason looked at him. "We be acting like shit over when it ain't. That's our problem. We gotta always be on our toes with them niggas."

"Maybe. But today we celebrate. Tomorrow we fight."

"As long as Dennis alive, ain't nothing to celebrate about."

Linden sighed. "What about the girl?" He nodded at the house.

Mason glared. "What about her?"

"If you want the war over, maybe you should give her back," Linden shrugged. "I know you had her call him and tell him the relationship was done over the phone."

Mason smiled. "Fucking with his head."

"I get all that...but giving Nikki back could stop all this shit."

"Who said I wanted the war over?"

"It's been five years since I got to know you," Linden took a sip of beer and sat it on the ground. "And I know losing Pops fucked up your head but I feel like it's something else." He burped. "Like part of your heart is with us but the other half ain't."

"What you trying to say?"

"Maybe you really fuck with Banks and—"

"You not saying nothing I wanna hear." Mason waved him off. "And I'm not letting her go 'til I get ready." He pointed into his chest.

Linden nodded. "Then—"

POP! POP! POP! TAT! TAT! POP! TAT! TAT! POP! POP! POP! TAT! POP! TAT!

Suddenly gunfire poured into the crowd in front of the yard. With a quick glance, it was easy to see where the firepower originated. The cars lined in front of the house looked innocent enough but instead contained deadly killers inside...Wales soldiers, who were eager to make their mark and enact revenge.

They emptied clip after clip into the crowd from opened windows sending Lou soldiers falling to the ground, their blood watering the earth. When gunfire ceased, and all clips were empty, ten cars sped away from the house, leaving free parking spaces in their wake.

Mason and Linden jumped up, ran toward the curb and released their hammers. They fired into the direction the cars drove into but it was too late. The hitters were long gone and the damage was done. Leaving twenty corpses behind, spread out on the lawn like dead branches.

Including their most trusted man, their brother Kevin.

Linden rushed up to him, dropped to his knees and raised Kevin's head as he screamed, "NOOOOOOOO!"

After Pete was murdered, tension was heightened in the Wales organization. Inside a luxurious hotel,

Dennis paid one of the three soldiers that stood outside of their room and then locked the door. Taking a deep breath, he hobbled up to Banks who was planted in the middle of the floor. He was wearing black jeans and a black shirt, with dark shades covering his eyes.

"It worked," Dennis smiled.

"I knew it would." Banks walked over to the bar and made a drink inside their suite. Vodka poured onto ice in a glass until it almost eased out.

"But how did you know where they were?" Dennis asked him.

"Who did we hit?" Banks responded, ignoring his question, and taking a deep sip.

"From what I heard Kevin took two. One between the eyes. The other to the center of the chest."

"And...Ma...Mason?" Banks took a large gulp. "They get him too?"

Dennis glared. "When are you gonna stop this shit?"

"What now?" Banks drank all of his drink and poured another before flopping on the edge of the bed.

"I know you still consider him a friend, Banks. The thing is, he ain't."

"What you trying to say?"

"I feel like your men could've gotten him too." He paused. "But I'm made to believe you instructed them to keep him alive."

"Too much has happened for me ever to consider him a friend." He paused. "You saw to that when you killed Arlyn."

"Then why did you hold off on telling me that you knew where they were?"

"Because you reckless, Pops." He paused. "And when I found out the other day where he lived, my plan was to make sure Nikki wasn't there first. But she dumped me and then they hit Pete so my plan was off. I wanted to move before they left the house."

"What you mean by calling me reckless?"

"I mean look around! Everybody in our family gone. I can't do shit how you want no more. From here on out we not killing niggas unless we sure."

"You step back in the game one day and now you the quarterback?" Dennis glared. "You think you telling me how things going in the organization I built?"

"You getting old. And your moves old too."

Dennis glared. "You disrespectful red ass—"

"I'M HERE!" Banks ran up to him, spit flying from his mouth. "YOU WANTED ME HERE AND NOW I'M ALL IN!" He pointed into Dennis's chest with a stiff finger. "BUT FROM HERE ON OUT WE DOING THINGS MY WAY!" Banks downed his drink, walked to the door and opened it. Within seconds three men stomped inside and surrounded Dennis. "Take him to his room." Banks ordered. "Stay with him. Make sure he remains safe."

Dennis' eyes widened. "Banks, what's going—" One of the men touched Dennis' arm to help lead him out, respectfully at first. "Get the fuck off me!" Dennis yelled.

They all grabbed him, ignoring his words. His cane dropped to the floor.

"What's going on?!" Dennis continued. "Banks, tell me something."

"I'm retiring you." Banks said sipping his drink. "Don't worry. You'll still live the good life."

They dragged him out the suite, kicking and screaming the entire way.

CHAPTER TWENTY-ONE
WEEKS LATER

Mason had developed a love of a crowd. And at the moment all eyes were on him, inside of his basement, as he made his canvas red. The vividness of the paint shined against the white material before thickening and hardening into a dark brown paste.

"I can't believe you doing this shit, man," Linden said, grossed out. He was amongst ten of their soldiers who got off on seeing Mason create. Far from impressed, instead he was horrified. "We could've used her a bit longer. But you go kill the one person we could've negotiated for. Nikki being dead ain't helping us one—"

"This is how you wanted me," Mason said pointing his bloody brush at him. "Remember? I was too soft to hear you tell it. Well that ain't me no more."

"I'm just—"

"Are you scared, Linden?" Mason asked with a lowered brow. "Because scared niggas don't need to be nowhere 'round me."

Linden sighed deeply. "You know I'm the last person to scare."

Mason dipped his brush into the open flesh of Nikki's gut as she lie dead on the table, dampening his tool yet again. Dead a long time ago, the liquid that once kept her alive, was now being used to create dark art.

"This gonna push things to the next level with the Wales'," Linden said. "You know that right?"

Mason smeared more blood onto the canvas. "Then let shit get pushed. He killed my brother. Now it's time for Banks to step to me."

Banks sat in the backseat of a black Lexus with tinted windows. Chains hung from his neck as he was chauffeured to the house he bought for him and Nikki to spend the rest of their lives inside. But when she went missing, he never visited the property, wanting instead to experience the moment with her.

But after hearing her say she didn't want him any longer, he realized it was time to move on. Not only that, he hadn't completed all of his paperwork and today was the final day or he would risk losing his deposit and home.

"Well where is he?" Banks asked as he talked into his cell phone.

"I don't know, sir."

"I told you to keep eyes on him," Banks said through clenched teeth. "At all times. I gave specific orders and now you telling me he shook you again?"

"We won't let anything happen to your father, sir."

"Don't tell me what you not gonna let happen. Find Dennis!" Banks snapped. "Now!" He hung up.

Banks loved his father, he truly did. But lately he felt like his reckless behavior was causing them too much drama. What was the use of having money when there was no way to spend it? At the end of the day Banks felt locked up and he needed to get control of his pops, and hopefully save their relationship at the same time, if they were ever going to survive.

When they pulled up to the gate in front of Banks' mansion, it opened and he nodded at the five men who covered the entrance. After Pete was murdered, Banks bumped up security but he also realized they couldn't be with him everywhere and as a result he had to keep his guards up at all times.

When the car parked in front of his house, he got out and walked into the front door. Peering around, he nodded at three of his men who were inside waiting. All had their weapons in hand, ready to act immediately if gunplay kicked off. But it was the large painting covered with a brown paper bag wrapping that sat in the middle of his living room floor that caught his attention.

One of his soldiers walked over to him. "Hello, Mr. Wales."

"How this get in my crib?" Banks asked pointing at it.

"A delivery truck came earlier."

"And?" Banks glared.

"We didn't let them in, but we brought it inside. Figured it was yours."

Banks glared harder. "Well I ain't order shit!" He stepped up to him. "So it shouldn't be here!"

"Sorry, sir."

"Fuck sorry! You open it!" Banks pointed in his face.

"Sir?"

"Open the fucking package," Banks said through clenched teeth.

"Yes, sir." He cleared his throat, tucked his gun behind him, lowered his height and tore at the brown paper revealing one sentence written in blood on the canvas.

By T. STYLES

CHAPTER TWENTY-TWO

Dennis walked up to the carryout counter drunk and swaying far more than a man who was worth millions should. He was getting stares from onlookers who wondered what the flashy man with the gold and diamond cane had consumed in his gullet to make him so wasted.

After somehow managing to place an order, Dennis waddled over to a young woman with long silky hair that ran down her back. She had been looking at him seductively ever since she laid eyes on him.

"Hello, hell..." He swayed a little but regained his stance. "Hello there."

She giggled. "Are you okay? You seem out of it."

He smiled, his breath bringing with it the odor of many bottles of vodka and rum. "I will be if you'll join...if you can..." He stumbled backwards and then rushed forward with his head, stopping right before hitting her. It was as if it were too heavy. "If you can join me for dinner."

"Now why would I do that?" She asked, licking her lips.

He smiled. "Don't...don't let the...fool you I'm...I can handle my liquor."

"So that's what you had." She giggled. "Liquor?"

"Come on, sweet thing, don't make me beg."

"Mr. Dennis," the carryout cashier yelled. "Your food ready."

He waved the cashier off as if she was annoying and focused back on the woman before him. She looked good enough to eat. Or at the very least fuck. "What can I do to convince you to come with me...right now?"

She gazed him over. "Let me get my food and then we'll see."

Five minutes later they were sitting inside his brand new black BMW. The smell of steak and cheese in the air. The moment the door was closed, Dennis placed his cool thick hand on her thigh preparing to crawl upward, into her panties and inside her pussy with his soiled fingernails. Since he hadn't bathed in days.

"Slow down, sweetheart," she said stopping his paws from going forward. "Everything in time."

"But you in my car now." He frowned. "What I gotta wait for?"

"Because you didn't give me a chance to show you this." She smiled, before easing a small .22 handgun from her purse. "That's why."

Initially Dennis was too inebriated to see the weapon aimed at him. But after blinking several times, it was apparent that the eye of the gun was in his direction. This woman had something else in mind.

"Wait a minute, beautiful," he said holding up his hands. "Ain't no need to take things this far. I was just playing with you."

"You see that's where you're wrong. There is a lot of need."

He swallowed the lump forming in his throat.

Shit was dire.

Banks warned him time after time to be careful and he avoided each of his pleas. Even down to refusing to stay in the hotel room where he could be protected from the enemies of the street. Without a doubt Dennis had allowed his pride to disregard his son's final orders and now it appeared as if he'd have to pay for it, maybe with his life.

"So you gonna rob me?" He frowned. "Is that what the...is that what the fuck you want?"

Slowly her pretty face morphed into an evil monster. She even looked much older than the youth he gave her when he first laid eyes on her face. "I don't want your money."

"Then what do you want?" He yelled.

"What do you think?"

Banks sat at a card table with Bet Stanley, real estate agent and interior decorator, sitting across from him. Three of Banks' men stood behind him as the final documents needed to make the mansion he purchased officially his were signed. If only Bet wasn't so attractive, he could focus on the papers before him but she was breathtaking and in a way that made him despise her.

She was throwing him off his chi.

Although Banks acted as if her beauty wasn't real, his men couldn't help but feel some kind of way. Her light brown skin, shoulder length black bob hair cut, thick pink lips and voluptuous body she was hiding under the navy blue business skirt was a dream come true.

And still Banks made a firm decision...to swear off all women and get on with life.

Bet on the other hand had other ideas.

From the moment she sold him the property, she was taken by how handsome he was. And now that a five o'clock shadow had covered his face, she wanted him even more, but how could she get his attention? He didn't seem interested in the least.

His tall lanky body, the cool way he moved and even the money he obviously had at his disposal, all had her wondering what she needed to do to be a part of his world. Bet's panties were moist just thinking about the possibilities.

By T. STYLES

But first she needed to know if there was a Mrs. Wales.

"That's it," Bet said sticking the papers back into the manila folder. She clutched her manicured nails together and looked across the table at Banks. "For now anyway. Do you have any questions?"

"Nah." He pushed the chair back and stood up, eager to leave her presence. Business with her was officially over but there was still other matters on the street he was certain were waiting for him.

"So do you think Mrs. Wales would love it here?" She asked looking up at him.

"Excuse me?"

"I...uh...remember you said you were purchasing this for your fiancé."

Banks shook his head and walked toward the staircase.

Bet stood up, embarrassed by his cold manner. "Mr. Wales, when will you be furnishing your home?" Bet yelled before he could disappear. "Because I have access to—"

"That's the last thing on my mind." He looked at his soldiers. "Show Ms. Stanley to the door."

He walked away, two of his men following, the other escorting her out of the premises.

Once upstairs he sat on the only piece of furniture in the room, his bed. While two men stayed outside because Banks took security serious and never thought he was fully safe, even in his own home. He was just about to kick his sneaks off and take a nap when his phone rang.

Slowly he stood up and walked across the room. Grabbing the wireless handset sitting on the floor, he listened first.

"Boss."

Recognizing the voice behind the call he ran his hand down his face. "Yeah...what's up?"

"Got bad news."

Banks sighed. "He's dead."

"Yes, sir." The caller paused. "Is there anything I can do for you?"

"Be at my house in an hour." He took a deep breath. "I wanna talk to you about a few things."

Two hours later Stretch Denney showed up at Banks' mansion and was escorted inside. The moment Stretch was given orders to show up, he felt things were about to change for the better in his life. Stretch had been trying to increase his ranks in the Wales' organization for years and now with everyone around Banks being dead, he hoped a new opportunity for him would arise. He wanted the chance to prove his loyalty so badly, some even joked that he resembled Banks, even down to his tall lanky body and light skin.

Honored to be in his presence, Stretch stood in the middle of the floor and Banks approached him. "Come

By T. STYLES

with me." When two of Banks' men followed, Banks addressed them. "This private."

The soldiers nodded and walked back to the foyer, as Banks and Stretch entered a more private room off to the right. Which would later become his office. When the door was closed Banks took a deep breath. "I want you to set up a meeting."

"Sure." Stretch nodded. "With who, sir?"

"Mason Lou." He paused. "Don't call him...find him. And I want you to keep this private."

Stretch sighed.

This was a moment in his mind that could change everything. To bite his tongue and not share his angst for Banks' meeting with a lifelong enemy, could put Stretch in a position to be only an errand boy. But Stretch wanted more and felt he needed to speak the truth or risk his future forever.

"Boss, I don't know about this." He paused. "We don't know who killed Dennis and—"

"I appreciate your honesty but I know what I'm doing." Banks placed a firm hand on his shoulder. "Set up the meeting. Let me worry about the rest."

Banks walked toward the door.

"Any conditions?" Stretch asked.

Banks turned around and faced him. "Yeah. Tell him to come alone."

It was a little chilly but Banks was exerting energy as he stood at the basketball court shooting hoops. Within two minutes of the scheduled time, Mason walked up to him wearing oversized black basketball shorts. He was alone. The two stood in front of each other and stared for what seemed like forever.

"You getting old, nigga," Mason said. "Hair all over your face and shit."

"And you getting fat," Banks said, pointing at his gut.

"You got me fucked up." Mason chuckled. "This all muscle over here." He stared at him for a bit longer and hit the ball out of Banks hand. "You don't want that shit!"

Mason ran around the court as Banks gave chase. They went shot for shot, racking up a score of eighty-to-eighty before they both realized one thing, there was no beating the other. At the end of the day they were equally matched and it was as simple as that.

Exhausted, Banks sat on the court with his back against the fence.

Mason sat next to him, both men looking outward at the empty court.

"What you want?" Mason asked. "I know you ain't call me here to shoot no hoops."

"My men told me not to come." Banks responded. "Said it would be dangerous."

"And as usual you ain't listen." Mason laughed. "You as bad as me. Linden would snap if he knew I was here."

Banks chuckled before growing quiet. "I'm tired of the war." He paused. "I wanna put an end to it right now."

Mason nodded. "Things gone too far." He looked at him. "You know that."

"That's what they say." Banks paused. "But is that what you believe?" He stared at him and awaited an answer.

Mason wiped sweat away from his forehead with the back of his hand. "Why didn't you reach out? And say something? After my father died?"

Banks brought his knees closer to his chest. "I didn't know what was going down, man. I was just a kid." He laughed. "Some of the niggas around me believe I'm still one now."

"But...why didn't you reach out?" Mason asked more passionately. "You knew he was all I had and...we were friends."

Banks nodded. "You right." He shrugged. "I guess I couldn't believe it was happening."

"But I fucked with you. Even vouched for you to my family. For the longest. And you had me looking crazy to my brothers."

Banks nodded. "If I could've stopped it I would have."

Mason looked down. "Did you see...did you see how it happened? With Pops?"

"Do you really wanna know?"

Silence.

"So now what?" Mason asked, taking his lead and deciding it was best not to know every detail about Arlyn's demise.

Banks sighed. "I heard you in the murder business."

"That's evident," Mason boasted, secretly reminding him of all those he killed, including the love of his life.

"Be careful with me," Banks warned. "I'm not the same kid you knew back in the day. A lot has changed."

"I'm not the same either," Mason retaliated.

"Then respect will keep us honest. And alive."

"Indeed." Mason nodded.

"I know you want out the murder business," Banks continued. "The streets been talking." He paused. "Plus it's not gonna give you the longevity you desire. I'm in a position to change your life."

"How?"

"I circulate coke on the coast. And I wanna put you on."

"Nidia gonna deal with you?"

"Yes. I'm not a Lou."

Mason frowned. "Why would you do that?"

"Because I wanna get on with the business of making money." He paused. "I mean if you wanna carry this gangsta shit on for another five years I'm with that too. But when will it be enough? We in a position where we can end the war and get paid. Ain't that what it's about?"

Mason looked away. "I gotta talk to my team."

Banks stood up.

Mason rose too.

"I understand." Banks paused. "But if we gonna do...if we gonna do anything..." Banks took a deep breath. "I'ma need the body."

"Nikki's?"

"Who else?" He glared. "I want to...I gotta do her right." He was doing his best to force back emotions. "She deserves that much."

"How you know I got her?" Mason asked.

Silence.

"I want the same." Mason continued. "For my father."

He nodded. "I think I can remember how to get back there," Banks said.

Mason sighed. "I didn't kill your father. I wanted to but I didn't put that work in."

Banks nodded. "I know. Because I did."

He bopped away and Mason's jaw hung.

"Let me know what you gonna do," Banks continued. "You got twenty-four hours."

Banks watched as two of his men placed the last granules of dirt over Nikki's body on a piece of land he purchased when he made his first million. There were no houses or dwellings within miles...just acres upon acres of greenery.

Mason stood next to him. And when the grave was complete, the Wales and Lou soldiers walked away leaving Banks and Mason alone.

"Did she suffer?" Banks asked him staring at the newly covered earth.

Mason glanced at him. "You know me." He paused. "What do you think?"

Banks sighed. The rage he was feeling had him rethinking the entire business deal to put the war away, along with his bitter feelings. At the same time he knew in his heart that he didn't want to live like this anymore.

At the end of the day Dennis was right.

Banks wanted power.

And he was making smart moves to make it happen.

So placing his feelings aside, Banks made a decision that he didn't want to know the details. Instead he would make sure Nikki's life wouldn't end in vain and he would be the best man he could. Yes he thought about what would've happened if she never moved from Minnesota, to Baltimore and met him. But that was the past and it was time to move on.

So he did. But she would always be in his heart.

The next day Banks went with Mason to the place Dennis buried his father. Both were holding bottles of beer, after drinking all day while looking at the earth, heavy with grass and flowers. In the beginning Mason was going to have Arlyn moved but after seeing the serenity of the unmarked grave next to the oak tree, he elected to keep him where he was, while saying a few words.

"Dad, I know you ain't want this for your life," Mason said. "And I know you ain't want the things I've been doing for mine either. But I'm trying to..." Mason sighed. "I'm trying to be better. And for some reason I think I'm gonna be okay." He looked over at Banks. "Rest in peace pops...I got you."

He poured liquor over the grave, where flowers and weeds had grown over the years since Arlyn had been buried.

When he was done they both walked toward Banks' ride.

"I'm in." Mason said softly.

Banks smiled and both paused and used the moment to shake hands. "Then let's get this money. Together."

CHAPTER TWENTY-THREE

Banks walked into Nidia's mansion in Houston, Texas, with three of his men guarding him. Stretch being among them. The moment they entered the elaborate living room, Gary walked up to him with his arms behind his back. He had Carl, the white man with red pimples throughout his face, at his side.

Gary extended his hand. "I'm Gary. What's your name?"

Banks shook his hand. "I'm Banks." He looked behind Gary. "Is...is Nidia here? We have a meeting." He looked at the watch on his arm.

"Actually she's waiting for you upstairs." Gary smiled.

Banks gazed at Stretch and back at Gary. "I'd prefer to meet down here." He paused. "That is...if it's cool with her."

Gary and Carl frowned. "What you mean you prefer to meet down here?"

Banks swallowed the lump in his throat, sensing he said the wrong thing. "Listen, I don't mean any disrespect...but I'd prefer...you know...to meet some place down here." Banks remembered when his father said to never go upstairs. The last thing he wanted was to be in a position where he would have to fuck her. In his opinion it was all about the money.

After taking in Banks' statement, Gary whispered in Carl's ear and Carl walked away. Minutes later he returned with six men. Since the Wales soldiers were unarmed upon entry, they immediately overcame Banks' men with a few blows to the head with collapsible batons.

"What the fuck is going on?" Banks asked as he was dragged kicking and screaming into the backyard. Thick blood rolling down his light skin. After a few quick seconds, Banks was knocked to the ground and a gun was pressed to the back of his head by one of the six.

"What are you doing here?" Gary asked through clenched teeth.

"What do you...what do you mean what am I doing here?" Banks' entire body trembled as he stood on his knees. "I'm here because...because I have a meeting with—"

"WHAT ARE YOU DOING HERE?" Gary yelled louder, spit escaping his mouth. "WHO THE FUCK SENT YOU?"

As quickly as things changed, it was apparent to Banks that he was in a room full of mad men. One minute he was at Nidia's residence to talk about the future of coke and the next he was on his knees with a gun to his head, wondering if he would survive.

Realizing that there was nothing he could do, he calmed his breath. If he were going to die it would be with dignity. "I'm here to talk about the coke. Nothing more. But I ain't about to beg. Do whatever you want."

Silence.

"Let him go." A woman said softly. "Now."

When Banks was helped up and turned around, he saw Nidia standing behind him. As calm as a windless sea. She was wearing a long black silk negligee and a matching robe and her arms were crossed over her chest.

Banks wiped the blood and sweat off his face. "Can you tell me what's going on, Nidia?" He asked softly. "Because I'm not understanding. You told me to meet you here."

"I don't answer questions. I ask them."

Silence.

"I heard about your father." She continued. "And I must admit, I'm getting tired of various members of the Wales family altering my business interactions."

"I'm sorry about that too...there was nothing we could do to protect him."

"Is that right?" She glared as if she knew more.

"Yes."

She looked him up and down, and he could tell she was angry because he elected not to meet her in her room, as she clearly preferred. "So is it true? That you're getting into business with the Lou's?"

"Nothing is finalized." He paused. "Not yet anyway."

She nodded. "As long as you know I will never, *ever*, work with them directly," she paused. "They are a hapless bunch of thugs and are bad for business. You'll find out soon enough."

Banks nodded.

"I guess we can try to continue." She pointed at him. "With the same terms. Your father being dead won't stop my product from circulating. I hope you know that. I expect the same level of distribution."

"I understand."

She took a deep breath. "Collect your men and get the fuck out my house." She said. "Expect your next delivery tomorrow."

"But we good until a few weeks from—"

"If you can't handle deliveries we can't do business." She paused. "Make your decision now."

Banks nodded. "I'm...we're in."

She glared and walked away.

CHAPTER TWENTY-FOUR

Banks stood up and looked around the large boardroom table in a building he rented in Landover, Maryland. On the left were the Louisville clan and on the right was the Wales clan.

Mason sat on Bank's direct left and Stretch on his right.

"I've called you all here because it's time to make money," Banks said looking out amongst the throng. "And it's time to do that now."

Linden laughed under his breath. "No offense, but we been doing alright, young nigga," he paused. "I don't see no reason we should start working together now."

"So you like bloodshed?" Stretch asked him. "Because we can do more of that if you in the mood."

Every man in the room grabbed their guns and was ready to display them to the board until Banks raised his hand. "Nobody is questioning anybody's dick size so put the fucking weapons down." He paused. "NOW!"

Everyone complied.

"This meeting is about one thing...getting paper," Banks continued.

"How do we know we can trust you?" Linden asked. "You took out my entire family." He looked at his brother. "Me and Mason are all we got."

"And we hit most of theirs too," Mason reminded his only living sibling. "Ain't a person on either side of our family without dead soldiers."

Linden glared at his flesh and blood.

"To be correct, I lost *all* of my family," Banks said. He took a deep breath. "War has a tendency to carry over into the future if no one is willing to put aside ill will. Yes, we can drag this out for years. You can kill our men. We can kill many more of yours but why?"

Mason looked at Banks.

"As it stands now money is being made but you can't spend it because everyone is looking over their backs," Banks continued.

"I got one question!" Linden said through clenched teeth. "Did you kill Arlyn?"

"No. But my father did." Banks paused. "And for his crime I took his life."

The room grew loud, everyone talking under their breath amongst themselves. Outside of Mason, no one knew about the crime until that moment. Mason didn't even tell Linden, being good at keeping secrets. The Wales organization was definitely shocked and the evil Banks was capable of was on full display at the moment.

"How do we know you're telling the truth?" Linden asked.

"I vouch for him." Mason said. "That's how you know."

Linden shook his head. Mason's ongoing loyalty to Banks was gross at best and he was tired of the bond they appeared to have shared. He knew there was more to their friendship and yet he couldn't find out what.

"I have no reason to lie," Banks responded. "And I'm not proud of what I did either. But it was a decision I made to ensure the future we wanted would be realized. It's just sad my pops wasn't here to see it. But he made reckless moves and so he had to go. Now I'm inviting you all along, right now, but you'll only get this moment." He pointed at each man at the table. "Refuse my charity and you can walk away, and we can carry out on some murder shit."

Silence.

"What we get out of it?" Linden asked.

"I am extending my access to cocaine," Banks continued. "And you will buy exclusively from me at a more than reasonable rate." He paused. "A rate so competitive you'll force other dealers to water down their product just to catch up."

"So you gonna sell to them too?" Linden asked.

"I'm a businessman. If they find me, which is not always easy, of course I'll sell to them. But never at the Lou rate. That's my guarantee." He paused. "If this works, like I know it can, in a very short amount of time you'll all be millionaires."

Mason rubbed his hands together just thinking about the possibilities.

"If we trust you, and you do us wrong again, there will be no more truce," Linden said.

"If I trust you, and you do us wrong, there will be gunplay like you can't imagine," Banks responded. "I'm talking a metal rainstorm. I promise you that." He glared at him.

Stretch grinned.

"So I guess we have an understanding," Linden said nodding his head.

"Good!" Mason said clapping his hands once. "It's time to get paid!"

Linden glared at his brother's excitement.

Suddenly five women came out holding trays filled with champagne in flutes. Every man present grabbed a glass. "Let us toast."

Everyone rose to their feet.

"To the future," Banks said. "May we all reach our heights and let nothing come between this family again." He paused. "Salud!"

The moment Mason walked into the house and closed the door Linden rushed up to him like an angry

By T. STYLES

girlfriend. The only thing missing was his bonnet. "If you ever go against me again in public I'm walking!" He pointed in his face. "Do you hear me? 'Cause I'm not fucking around!"

"Then walk now, nigga!" Mason yelled. "You act like I'm holding you back."

Silence.

Linden stepped away and paced a little. Taking a deep breath he approached his little brother again. "You never gave a fuck about anything but that nigga. Why? Did ya'll fuck or something?"

Mason stole him in the jaw and shook his hand when his knuckles throbbed.

Linden laughed and wiped the corner of his mouth. "Wow...maybe you did."

"You don't believe that." Mason continued to shake his hand.

"Then what *is* going on?" Linden yelled. "You made a decision to get into business with a man who killed all of our brothers and our father. Don't you feel bad about any of it? At all?"

"Why you want to live in the past, man?" Mason paused. "Huh?"

"It ain't about the past." He touched his bloody mouth again. "It's about you not thinking straight."

"Then what's your plan, Linden?" Mason flopped on the sofa and threw his hands up in the air. "I wanna hear it. Right now."

"It's not about having a plan."

"You in my face, yelling like a female about me choosing his side," Mason continued. "So I'm asking you right here and now what's your plan? If you have any plan, just one, I'll follow you. I swear to God I will."

Silence.

"Exactly," Mason continued, taking off his shoes.

"How you know he's not waiting?" Linden continued. "For the right moment to finish what he started with us? Doesn't this seem just a little suspicious? He has all the power and yet he wants to share it with a nigga who killed his family and bitch?"

"He murdered his own father." He paused. "To prove how much he wanted peace. With us."

"The nigga had too!" He yelled, spit flying like a sprinkler from his mouth. "I'll give Banks one thing, he realized we weren't letting up until we had his head. So he served up his own father on a platter. And that sounds like a man you trust?"

"That makes me trust him even more." Mason said. "Banks just trying to get this money and I'm trying to move somewhere that I'm not embarrassed to bring a bitch to." He paused. "Pops was in the streets, Linden. He knew what it was about. He knew he could meet his end and that's what happened. Soldiers die on the battlefield all the time."

"You secretly hated him didn't you?"

"Why you say that?"

"What happened with his brother?" Linden asked. "One minute he was alive and the next he—"

"Why you bringing him up all of a sudden?"

"Because some people say he was raping you. And that you hated Arlyn for it, because he didn't protect you. If that's true, then it makes sense why you don't care that Dennis killed him."

"What you wanna do?" Mason paused trying not to let him get to his mind. "'Cause I'm siding with money. What about you?"

"One day you'll realize he will always choose the best situation for him and not you." Linden continued. "I just hope I'm around to see it." He walked out of the house.

CHAPTER TWENTY-FIVE

Banks pulled up to his gate only to see Bet standing outside, holding a manila folder next to one of his armed men. She was wearing a black leather jacket, tight blue jeans that showed off her thick legs and fat ass, and a white Versace button up blouse that showcased her cleavage.

She was bad.

No lie.

"What up?" Banks asked, trying not to look too long into her pretty face. "What you doing at my house?"

She wiped her bangs out of her eyes. "I was...uh wondering if you could sign one more form."

"I thought I was done with all that shit."

"It's just one," she grinned.

He looked ahead through the gate at his house and then back at her. "Just...get in the car."

She happily slid inside as they pulled through the gate. Her expensive perfume caused him to get aroused and he wanted her away from him. Once inside the living room, she looked around because it was still empty. They walked toward a small table sitting in the middle of the room with two chairs.

"Banks, when are you gonna make this place a home?"

"What you mean?" He sat down.

By T. STYLES

"It's still empty." She looked around. "Except this table. Don't you want—"

"What you want?" Banks said, crossing his arms over his body. "You said you had some paper for me to sign, so where is it?"

"Huh?" She was so busy trying to get closer that she forgot about the nonessential document she brought that really didn't require his signature.

"You need me to sign something right?" He extended his hand. "Give it to me."

She sat across from him and slid over a form. "It's just a warranty. Basically if something happens within a year we'll cover the cost of repairs."

He nodded and signed. "Anything else?"

"Yes."

He shrugged. "What is it?"

"I was wondering if I could, maybe make you dinner or something?"

He smiled and shook his head. He knew something was up with this chick and now it was evident that he was correct. "I can get my own dinner."

"I know that but—"

"Boss, Mason is at the gate." One of his soldiers said.

"Let him in."

Banks got up and walked to the door. A few moments later Mason strolled inside and the second

Mason saw Bet his jaw dropped. "Damn, I didn't know you had company," he said eyeing Bet's body.

"It's not like that." Banks looked at Bet. "She was just leaving."

She smiled, stood up and walked over to Banks. "You don't like me now, I can tell, but you should know I don't give up easily." She shook Mason's hand. "My name is Bet and I'm sure I'll meet you again." She smiled and walked out.

Banks and Mason moved over to the table when she left.

"She bad as fuck," Mason said sitting down, looking at the door and back at him. "And you don't want that?"

"Not in the dating mood. Then again you know that already."

"Low blow."

Banks bit at the inside of his jaw. He didn't know what he wanted Mason to say in that moment but in his mind Mason never appreciated how much losing Nikki fucked up his plans. Not just as a couple but for life.

"What's up?" Banks asked.

"That chick gonna be your wife." He pointed at the door, totally off subject. "You know that right?"

"And you know that's not possible."

He shrugged. "Anything's possible." He paused. "But look, we ran out of the pack you gave us already. Need another."

Banks smiled. "So shit working out?"

"Better than I thought, man," Mason grinned. "Like we can't keep the shit in. You think it's possible to up the weight?"

"I can get whatever you need." He paused. "Trust me."

"Cool, then let me get back to the house and tell my team."

Mason stood up to leave but Banks walked over to him. There was something on his mind he wanted to talk to him about. "I been hearing some things...that I don't know if they're true."

"Ask away."

"They calling you a serial killer on the streets." Banks laughed, although he was seriously interested.

Mason glared. "Who told you that?"

"Don't matter." Banks shrugged. "But I addressed the nigga quick for even feeling comfortable enough to say shit to me about it. But is it true?"

"What part you hearing?"

Banks looked away. "The painting you gave me...was it...in blood?"

Silence.

"I gotta go, man," Mason said slapping Banks' chest with the back of his hand.

Banks moved closer. "We getting money together now. I need you to remember that while you're making moves out in the street. That's the problem I had with my father. And it's the problem Nidia had with Arlyn too. We need to look at the bigger picture."

"Whatever I do for extracurricular won't come back on you." Mason shook his hand. "You can believe that."

"I hope so."

Mason nodded and walked out.

Linden swaggered up to a group of three soldiers as they stood behind a strip club smoking weed. The moment they saw him, one of the men was about to drop the smoke on the pavement but Linden stopped them by waving his hand.

"That's not necessary." Linden said. "Give me that."

Oden handed it to him. "Sorry, man. We were waiting on you and Mason to come out."

"You sure about that?" Linden pulled on the weed and held it securely in his lungs. "Cause it look like you were getting high to me." He blew out smoke.

Oden looked at the others.

By T. STYLES

"Fuck all that," Linden said. "I got a job for you."

"Sure, man. Anything." Oden was eager to do whatever necessary to increase his position in the Lou's gang. Before he even knew the consequences.

"Are you sure 'bout that?" Linden continued, throwing the weed on the ground, even though it was still meaty. "Because once I tell you what I want ain't no turning back." He pointed at his face with a stiff long finger.

Oden looked at his peers and back at Linden. "Yeah, man, anything."

Linden nodded. "Good because you 'bout to be tested. Just hope you rise to the challenge." Linden gave them the details on his plan. When he was done he walked off, just as Mason strolled up to them.

"What was that about?" Mason asked Oden while watching his brother.

"N...nothing." Oden said as he stared at Linden getting into his car.

"Then why you looking all crazy?"

"No reason, man. I was just..." Oden shrugged again. "Nothing."

Mason nodded slowly. "Well let's bounce. I got something nice coming to the house for me. Ain't nothing in that place but hoes." He paused. "I need a bad bitch like yesterday."

"Sure, boss," Oden said as they all poured into the car.

CHAPTER TWENTY-SIX

The window was lowered as Banks was riding down the highway listening to the radio, thinking about his life. Things were falling in order but he still felt like something was missing. He slowed down when he saw a sign on a bulletin board that caught his attention.

LEARN TO FLY TODAY

Curious as a two-year-old, he quickly pulled off the exit, drove into the school and parked his car. As he walked through the lot he saw it was littered with small aircrafts and it made him more interested. Once inside the office, a cute white girl with fire red hair jumped up from her seat and smiled when she saw the handsome drug dealer ease inside.

He approached the counter. "What's the process...to...you know?" He pointed at the planes outside.

"No," she flirted, both rows of her pearly yellow teeth showing. "I don't know. What are you talking about? The process of getting my number or—"

"Flying." Banks said slapping his hand once on the counter. "I'm trying to learn how to fly."

The girl switched around the desk and hopped on top of it. Horny, she opened her legs wide so he could

By T. STYLES

see her pale pussy lips and thin red landing strip of strawberry colored hair. Her thighs were closed enough to pretend she wasn't being a freak but opened wide enough for him to know she wanted to fuck.

He did notice.

And wasn't impressed.

"You just have to fill out one of these forms." She reached back and grabbed an application, opening her legs a bit wider. "And then pay the fee." She handed it to him.

"What's the fee?"

"It's $2,000 but we can break that into smaller—"

"I can pay it," he said cutting her off. "In full. You got a pen?"

"Sure...sure," she cleared her throat.

It was obvious he wasn't interested so she plopped down off the table and pulled down her dress, hiding her pale thin cheeks. Next she handed him a black pen as she watched as he recorded his address on the form. When he was done he reached in his pocket and pulled out $2,500, separating it from the larger stack in his wad.

"Have the instructor call me tomorrow." He handed it to her.

"But we backed up on our list," she said; now dryer in her personality after realizing dick was off the table.

"That's why I'm giving you five to make it happen sooner." He paused. "I know you can do that." He kissed her cheek but not the one she wanted.

Still, suddenly, all was right in her slutty world. "I sure will."

DAYS LATER

Banks pulled up to the house and he was beat. His plan was simple, to get a shower, catch a nap and hit the streets. He had been gone for a few days visiting Nidia to re-up because with the Lou's in distro they couldn't keep the cocaine in Baltimore or the surrounding cities. Add to that he was pulling in more money than he could spend but he had a plan. A goal in mind, a number he kept written on a composition book that once was reached, he would knock out the next steps until he realized his dream.

The moment he drove up to his keypad to punch in his code, one of his men walked over to him. "It's really nice, sir."

Banks nodded, not knowing what he meant or caring. After driving into the gate, parking and walking into his house, he stumbled backwards, shocked when he realized his mansion was fully furnished and

By T. STYLES

carpeted. A black and white theme dominated the space, including the large cream leather sofa that sat in the center of the living room floor. Whoever designed it not only had taste but they captured the essence of what he wanted.

Still, he didn't purchase a bit of furniture.

Not a lick.

"Fuck is this?" He said to himself.

When he walked upstairs it was also completely embellished.

A massive king size bed sat in the middle of his room and it smelled of brand new furniture and carpet. Not a detail was left out. There were towels, washcloths and even pajamas neatly folded in dresser drawers.

Irate, Banks ran downstairs and outside the front door.

"Who the fuck was in my crib?" He snapped at his men standing next to the door. Looking like a bunch of bitches.

"I...I..."

"Who was in my house?" Banks yelled, gripping one of their shirts with both hands, raising a grown man off his feet.

"I don't know." He paused. "Want me to ask the day shift?"

Angry, he slammed the front door and stormed back into the house. Standing in the middle of the floor he called Mason and waited for an answer. "What up?"

"Did you decorate my crib?" Banks asked.

Mason laughed heavily into the phone. "What, nigga?"

"Did you or not?"

"Fuck I look like?" Mason snapped. "I ain't even decorate my own shit yet."

Banks hung up in his face.

He was about to make another call when one of his men knocked on the front door. Irritated, Banks yanked it open. "What now?"

"Ms. Stanley is at the gate."

"Who?"

"The real estate agent."

"Yeah...let her in." Banks kept his focus on making phone calls until she walked inside and hung in the doorway. "What you want now?" He said to her as he continued to go through call after call looking for the masked decorator.

"How was your...your trip?" She asked softly.

"Listen, now ain't the time." He said while dialing another number. "Somebody been up in my house and—"

"Do you like it?"

"That ain't the point! I ain't give orders for none of this shit."

She grasped her hands together and looked down at her French manicured nails. "Was hoping that you did like it because...it was me."

Slowly his eyes widened and he stomped toward her, stuffing his phone into his pocket. "You put all this shit in my crib?" His nostrils flared as he peered at her.

She nodded. "Yes...but I...well I ordered it on my company's card. We do it sometimes for clients who have big budgets." She paused. "I figured if you saw how it could look you'd want the—"

"BITCH, YOU DON'T COME INTO MY HOUSE WITHOUT MY PERMISSION!" He gripped her by her blouse and pointed in her face. "ARE YOU FUCKING CRAZY?"

Bet trembled at how hard he was coming at her and tears began to roll down her cheeks. "No...I was just..."

"Get the fuck out!"

"I'm so—"

"Now!"

Bet was sitting on the side of the street crying her mascara down when Mason pulled up alongside her in his Benz. After Banks hung up he realized something was off so he decided to stop by to find out what had caused his long lost friend so much distress. But after seeing Bet he wanted to check her out first.

Besides, she was easy to look at if he was being honest.

Mason parked, exited his ride and knocked on the driver's side window, scaring her at first. "You okay?"

She shook her head no.

"Unlock the door." He pointed at it.

She glanced at him and Mason slid inside. "What happened?

"I...I had his house decorated and he..." She broke into heavy sobbing again.

"You gotta cut out all the crying and tell me what's going on," he paused. "I'm not understanding you right now."

She sniffled and wiped away her tears. Her eyes resembled a raccoon's. "I wanted to do something nice for him...so when he was gone, on vacation, I had his house decorated."

Mason knew Banks wasn't on vacation since he had to re-up but he appreciated her use of vernacular. "So you went in his crib without him knowing? And bought a rack of shit you expect him to pay for?"

She nodded.

He shook his head. "Listen, that's the last thing you wanna do with a man like Banks."

By T. STYLES

"I wasn't trying to be rude. I only wanted to—"

"It don't matter. Too much be going on to have any old person in our houses. We gotta be smart and that starts with knowing who comes in and out where we rest our heads."

"What does he...what does he do?" She paused. "For a living?"

Mason leaned back in the seat and the leather groaned. "Come on, B. You way smarter and prettier than that." He smiled. "I can see it in your eyes."

She took a deep breath. "Does he have somebody in his life?"

Mason thought about when he painted a few canvases with Nikki's blood. "Nah. Not anymore."

"So do you think he could ever like me?"

After firing the entire squad who guarded his house while he was at Nidia's, Banks paced the living room floor before finally sitting down on the large comfortable sofa. It wasn't until that moment that he realized how nice everything was. The rage he felt from Bet's disrespect had him ticking but now...now he was calming down and feeling a bit more relaxed. Still, she violated in the worst way.

When one of his newly placed soldiers approached him he looked up. "What now?"

"Mason at the door."

He sighed. "Let him in."

"I think he has company," he continued. "A lady."

Banks didn't know why but for some reason he felt relief. "Let both of 'em in."

Banks stood up and walked to the door, arms behind his back.

Within minutes Mason bopped in first and gave him some dap. "Where the rest of your niggas at?"

"Gone."

"I don't blame you." Mason paused. "But...uh look...I think I found something of yours outside," Mason looked at Bet. "But if you don't want it I'll—"

"Let me talk to her," Banks said softly. "Alone."

Mason winked and walked out.

"Listen, I'm sorry about...you just can't...I mean..." He took a deep breath and closed his door. "I don't know you like that to do something like this."

"I understand."

"Do you?" He paused. "I'm not the kind of dude who can have just anybody in his house. I have to be...I have to be careful, Bet. A lot be going on in my life."

She stepped closer.

Almost too closely for Banks' comfort.

He took one step back putting more space between them.

"I'll never overstep my boundaries again..." she took a deep breath. "I just...there's...there's something about you that I like and I don't know why. I haven't even been in a relationship because I'm a dreamer...maybe like my mother. She's been married to my father for forty years. And I never forgot when she told me that it was love at first sight." She continued. "My father he's the most amazing man in the world and—"

"Bet...slow down."

"I'm serious...every man I've ever met it always ended badly because I was trying to find someone like my father and then I found you. I wanted you from the first time I laid eyes on you."

"The feeling ain't mutual."

"But it can be."

He walked away. What he did to his own father covered his mind and the guilt was heavy as she spoke about the love for hers. He wondered if she'd ever understand if he shared his secret. Banks loved Dennis. He truly did, but the situations he was putting Banks in had caused him to fight with his own best friend, to lose his family members and finally Nikki being killed.

She followed behind him.

"And I think, if you would give me a chance...just one...you'd learn to like me too." She shrugged. "Maybe even love me."

This woman was going harder than a baseball bat to a skull and it made him uncomfortable. Her beauty didn't match her desperation but if nothing else he definitely found her interesting.

"Why you single now?" He asked turning around to face her.

"I'm serious...I'm looking for that perfect man."

Banks laughed. "Well I'm far from perfect."

"In my eyes you are."

"So you expect me to believe you don't have anybody in your life that you fuck with? Nobody at all?"

"I'm waiting." She moved closer. "I swear to God I am." She paused. "So what about...what about you?"

"I lost somebody I..." Nikki's face flashed into his mind and it felt like he was cheating just being near Bet. "I like being single."

"But you're missing out." She paused. "On me," she said playfully. "Because if I'm right, which I think I am, I swear to God I'm made for you."

"You too pushy to be a female."

"And normally I'm not like this...but I haven't been so close to somebody I want so badly. If I don't act now I'm afraid you'll get away." She looked down. "But you're right, maybe I'll just go home." She turned to walk away.

He grabbed her fingertips. Softly.

She froze in place. Her heart pumping in her chest. Her pussy moistening at his touch.

She turned to face him and he released his hold. Taking a deep breath he looked around. "So how much all of this gonna set me back?"

"I charged a little over seventy thousand on my company's credit account."

Based on the way he acted earlier, she expected him to be irritated; instead he walked away and returned with eighty thousand dollars in a duffle. He kept a bag on hand at all times for moments like this. "I put a little extra in there for you." He paused. "For the trouble."

She smiled and sat it by the door. "Thank...you...you didn't have to do that."

"I wanted to." He sighed and looked around. "And it's kinda nice in here."

She smiled.

"Real nice," he continued. "You did a good job. So...uh...you hungry?"

She nodded yes.

"I would offer you some food but I ain't been shopping yet." He paused. "We could go out and—"

"You check your refrigerator?"

"Trust me, ain't nothing in there."

She smiled.

"You can't be serious." He said, after getting where she was going.

She grabbed his hand. "Let me cook for you," she led him to the kitchen and opened the completely stocked fridge. "I didn't know what you liked so I picked a little of everything." She paused. "I hope that's okay too."

CHAPTER TWENTY-SEVEN

Smoke filled the car as Mason trailed behind another vehicle in his brand new Lexus. He was slick too because *they* didn't know he was following. He spent all day moving into his new home in Pikesville Maryland and he was exhausted but couldn't rest. No time for sleep, after speaking to a few of his men he learned that there was more to be done, or a major move would be made without his authorization.

When his phone rang he put down his weed in the ashtray and answered. At the same time he was sure to keep his eyes on the car ahead of him. "What is it?"

"Where you?" Linden asked. "I been looking for you all day."

"Is that right?" Mason smirked as he merged to the left and then right.

"Fuck that's supposed to mean?" He paused. "Anyway I was just calling to let you know that one of our men was robbed last night."

"So take care of it." Mason shrugged. "You handle that part anyway."

"You know what...next time I won't tell you shit." Linden continued. "Every time I try to talk to you—"

"I gotta go," Mason said, hanging up in his face.

When the car he was trailing parked in an aviation lot, he passed it and stopped in an auto body shop on the next block instead. After paying some mechanics a few bucks to keep eyes on his ride, he crept to the lot on foot. Standing behind a parked plane, he saw Banks getting out of another that just landed, before walking into a building with a tall white man wearing a green aviation jacket.

He also spotted the car he was trailing, with two men inside, parked in the vehicle lot.

Slowly Mason walked up to the car and crawled inside. The moment the door shut, Oden and George jumped when they saw their boss behind them, glaring in their direction. When Mason gazed down to the left, he saw latex gloves, duct tape and rope on the seat next to him.

Oden's throat bubbled. "Hey...hey...boss...what you...what's going on?"

"So we gonna do this or not?" Mason asked rubbing his palms together.

Oden's eyes widened as he looked at George and back at Mason. "You with this?"

"Of course I am," Mason said nodding. "Nothing gets done without my say so." He looked at Banks who was talking to a white girl with red hair by the entrance of the building. "That nigga been on my radar for years. It's definitely time to kill him."

Oden nodded. "Good because I feel better now."

"Word." Mason said through clenched teeth, not caring about the man's feelings.

"Yeah." Oden scratched his scalp. "Cause Linden said not to let you know about this. Said you wouldn't want Banks gone but it was still best for business."

"And you didn't tell me." Mason nodded. "Good for you." He was trying not to allow his anger to swell inside of him but it was difficult. "So now all we gotta do is wait for Banks to come out and gut his ass."

Oden and George turned around to focus on Banks. The moment their eyes were off Mason, he jabbed a blade in the back of Oden's neck. Then he sliced George's throat on the side before he could get control of the shaky gun he was attempting to aim in Mason's direction. When he was done, and blood poured from both of their gaping wounds, he wiped the blade on the back of the seat and slid out the car.

"So how did you find out about the hit on him anyway?" Linden asked as he stood in the middle of an empty luxury apartment he rented a few weeks earlier.

"Oden was bragging that he was gonna be second in command to the boss," Mason said cracking his knuckles. "And he thought that would be you."

"Stupid ass niggas." Linden was angry that he hired idiots to do a man's job but now it was too late and his cover was blown. "I was trying to—"

"I don't give a fuck what you were trying to do!" Mason said rushing up to him. "I said not to make moves on Banks without my word! And you disobeyed me! Now he trying to figure out why two dead Lou niggas in the aviation parking lot."

"What you tell him?"

"That I ain't know 'em!" He paused. "Why you go off my word?"

"Your word?" Linden snapped. "You don't tell me what to do, lil' nigga!"

"See that's your problem. You don't understand chain of command. You still under the impression you in charge when you anything but!"

"We family."

Mason nodded. "I know...and that's why it's gonna hurt me to do this." He took a deep breath. "You cut."

Linden leaned forward. "Cut?"

"That's what the fuck I said." Mason stepped closer. "I'm not gonna let you or nobody else come in between me and my money."

"Wow. You a disloyal ass roach."

Mason stormed toward the door. "Whatever...you were warned."

Right before he exited Linden said, "You know I'm not gonna end stuff like this right?" Linden asked. "I don't care how long it takes. You have to be smarter than that, Mason. You know this ain't going to end well."

"You don't want it with me, big bruh." Mason warned. "You and me both know that." He walked out, slamming the door behind him.

Mason drove slowly down the street slopping up beer along the way.

He couldn't lie, he was in his feelings about cutting his brother off and at the same time he felt he couldn't be trusted. He needed him to know that things weren't going to run how they did in the past, when he was a kid. But Linden wasn't getting the message. He still thought he could move over his head without repercussions and Mason knew the future meant showing he was in charge.

High out of his mind, he was about to merge on the parkway when he saw a man fussing at his woman across the way. His wild hands flew over the woman's head and he thought he would hit her at any minute. Although he was far from a hero, something about the broad made him curious so he pulled over.

Easing out of his car, he walked up to the duo. "Something going on here?"

"Fuck you worried about it for?" The man yelled stomping up to him, hands clenched like two rocks.

"Terry, please don't," she said touching his arm.

"Bitch, shut the fuck up!" Terry yelled into her face before focusing back on Mason. "This little nigga should've minded his own business." He moved so close to Mason their belly's touched. "Now it's too late."

Mason smiled. "Indeed."

Banks woke up to the smell of bacon, eggs and biscuits cooking in the kitchen. Yawning, he opened his drawer, grabbed a pill bottle and popped a few into his mouth. After swallowing them, he walked downstairs to see what was going on. Since Bet slept in one of the newly decorated guest rooms, he figured she would be turned off after begging to lie in his bed all night, only to be turned down.

She wasn't.

"I figured you'd be hungry." She pulled out a chair and fixed him a plate with the works.

By T. STYLES

Afterwards she made her own and sat in front of him. "My father would love you," she grinned. "A lot." She paused. "I hope you like the food."

"If it's anything like the lasagna you made last night I'm sure I will."

"Do you even...like do you find me attractive?" She paused. "Or am I barking up the wrong tree? You can be honest and tell me the truth."

She was pushy but he looked up at her and could see the seriousness in her eyes so he decided to be real with her about a few things. Shoving his plate aside he took a deep breath. "I need to tell you something...if you're still here, I'll give this...whatever it is...a chance."

"Okay," she sat down. "I'm listening."

"But if you gone I won't take it the wrong way." He paused. "You already got your money and you can leave. No strings attached."

She moved her chair closer to him. "I'm listening, Banks. You can tell me anything."

An hour later, after revealing his secret, and leaving her to her thoughts downstairs, Banks was taking the longest shower of his life. Although it was only fifteen minutes, it seemed like forever when he had things on his mind. Once he got out and threw on a new pair of jeans he bought and a fresh white t-shirt, he tried to see if he could hear her moving downstairs.

He didn't. Besides, his mansion was too large for small sounds to carry.

Figuring it was time to face her, he walked downstairs. But the moment he bent the corner he saw the kitchen was clean and the food was put up.

More importantly Bet was gone.

CHAPTER TWENTY-EIGHT

The man's body lie on top of the table, open at the belly inside Mason's basement.

Hysterical, the man's girlfriend sat in a chair across the room, looking at what she deemed to be a madman using her ex-boyfriend's blood to paint a canvas. While he was creating sick art, she saw Mason pop a few pills into his mouth and watched as his eyes glassed over.

When Mason first pulled over to address the feuding couple, the woman thought it was to help. But within minutes her man was on the ground with a knife wound to the gut and Mason was demanding that she help him place his body into the trunk of her car. And now, instead of allowing her to leave, she was certain that he was holding her hostage.

"How long were you with this nigga?" Mason dipped his brush into the corpse's blood and stroked the canvas again.

Silence.

He looked back at her. "Hear me talking to you?"

She nodded and sniffled. "Uh...a...about six years."

He frowned. "You can't be no more than twenty yourself."

"I'm nineteen."

Mason glared down at the corpse. "So you were a kid too huh?"

"Too?" She paused. "You were raped?"

Mason took a deep breath and continued to paint. "I can never understand why niggas like this fuck kids and think shit's sweet." He paused. "The shit be messing me up." He took a deep breath and continued to paint in rage. "You free to go though. I ain't keeping you. Although I must warn you, tell no one what you've seen here tonight. If you know what's good for you."

Her eyes widened and she stood up slowly before moving quickly to the basement door, which led outside. Before walking out she turned around and looked at her dead boyfriend and then Mason.

"What?" He asked. "Why you still here?"

"I ain't got nowhere to go. No place to live."

"Ain't you scared?"

"Should I be?" She took a deep breath. "I stayed with him and he took care of me for most of my life." She cried. "He was...he was everything. And still I wanted him gone." She sobbed harder. "I wanted him gone so bad because he beat me everyday. He beat me repeatedly. And now that he's dead...I...I don't know what to do."

Mason looked at her a little longer. "What's your name?"

"Jersey."

He nodded. "Well, Jersey, if you ain't got no place to go, I guess you staying with me."

Banks held his cell phone to his ear as he rushed to the front door in his mansion. He missed a meeting because he overslept, something he normally didn't do. But the new medicine he was on fucked up his sleep wake schedule and would take some time to adjust. "I'm on my way right now. Just make sure you count the cash before I get there. I don't want my time wasted."

Rushing, he pulled the front door open and froze when he saw Bet standing there, waiting. Her hands were clutched in front of her and she was wearing a low-cut yellow dress and a black leather coat. Her bob hair blew in the wind. "You...are you about to go somewhere?" She pointed at her car. "I can leave and—"

"No..." he opened the door wider. "Come inside." He stepped back. "Please."

She complied and he closed the door behind her. "I'm sorry about leaving, Banks. It's just that...what you told me..."

"I understand." He paused. "You don't have to say anything else."

She stepped closer. "I went home and thought about it and even after what you said, I don't know what it is that draws me to you. I don't even know if it's a good thing."

"I get it."

She took a deep breath. "But if you allow me to, as a girlfriend at first, and then whatever later, I will make sure you have the life you deserve."

"But you don't know me."

"There is something about you, Banks." She paused. "And I want the chance to make life a little better. For us both."

He nodded. "If we gonna try we have to bypass some steps. Because who I am...what I'm about right now...I can't have you getting hurt out here."

"I'm not scared."

"But you should be." He put his hand over his chest. "Niggas will kill you just because you mine. Hold you for ransom and shit like that. So if we gonna be together I need you here, where I can make sure you safe."

"You want me to move in?"

Silence.

"Okay," she said.

He smiled. "Okay?"

"Whatever you want." She paused. "I mean look at this house." She looked up at the glowing chandelier and back at him. "It's amazing."

"And you can do this full time?"

"Yes. After I leave work I'll make sure—"

"You don't get it," Banks said stepping closer. "If you gonna be mine, you gotta be *all mine*. No work. No life outside of me. *Ever.*" He paused. "And I know it's messed up but that means keeping your father and mother away from what it is I do."

"My parents?" She paused. "And my job? But I've built a career that I deserve."

"I understand." He paused. "I do. But you in or what? 'Cause I gotta know now."

"Wow..."

Silence.

"Bet, you don't have to do anything you don't want. But before I invest in you I need you to hear me and know I'm not fucking around." He paused. "The door is right there...you can leave back out and I won't say a word. But once you gone ain't no coming back. This is it."

She looked down and took a deep breath. "Okay."

"You sure?"

"I am." She smiled. "And I'm gonna give you babies and a family and everything you ever wanted. All I ask is that you always be true and that you never make no decisions without me." She paused. "Deal?"

The woman was a maniac in his mind but he was feeling her. "You give it all up for me and I'll do right by you. That's my word."

She moved closer. "Guess we 'bout to build a dynasty."

"Guess we are."

The moment the lights were out, Jersey who was fresh out of the shower dropped to her knees. Loving her body, Mason walked up to her, reached down and helped her to her feet.

"What's wrong?" She whispered. "I want to make you happy."

"I just wanna...I wanna feel your body next to mine." He removed his shirt and pulled her warm body against his.

"I'll do whatever you desire." She said looking up into his eyes. "I promise."

He smiled. "Whatever?"

She nodded yes.

He pushed his jeans and boxers down. When he was completely naked he picked her up so that her legs straddled the sides of his body. Rock hard, he pushed into her pink tightness and moaned. "I want you to be my slave," he told her, pumping softly.

"Your slave?"

He nodded yes.

By T. STYLES

"O...okay." She smiled.

"Call me Master."

Already a submissive, and feeling the slow way he moved in and out of her body, she immediately warmed to the idea of him being in complete control.

"Master, will you...don't ever leave me."

He grabbed her ass cheeks and walked to the wall, so that her back was against it.

"Never disobey me. Never question me and I promise I'll always be...." When the pussy got wetter he smiled, immediately knowing she was a natural submissive. "Be there for you."

She wrapped her arms around his neck and twirled her waist until he splashed his cum into her waiting body.

The moonlight was just right as it shined on the Wales' mansion.

Slow music blared from the patio's speakers as Banks sat on a lawn chair smoking a cigar. A diamond studded chain rested on his black shirt and sparkled every time the wind blew across the crackling fire pit, causing it to dance.

When Bet's song came over the sound system, she slipped out of the pool wearing her skimpy red bathing suit. Standing at the exit of the pool she grinned at him.

"Damn you fine," he said as he admired her body from a far.

She winked at him and peeled off her dripping wet swimsuit and stood before him naked. Groping himself, he put down the cigar and blew out a huge cloud of smoke into the air. It hovered over his head and quietly disappeared into the ether.

"Get over here," he demanded.

Slowly she walked over to him, careful to make sure her ass jiggled and her titties bounced, something she knew turned him on.

Standing before him she pulled down his boxers and removed his thickness, before inserting him into her slick pussy. Loving the way her wet body slapped against his, he grabbed her waist and pumped harder.

Her head dropped backwards as he kissed her on the neck, sucking hard in an effort to leave his tracks. Banks got off on marking up her body, knowing when she walked out on the streets the world would know she was taken.

Right when she was about to cum, she planted her hands into Banks' chest and moved harder.

"Fuck me, Banks," she moaned. "Fuck this wet pussy."

Feeling himself about to bust he grabbed her waist harder and moved her up, down, left and right, so she could hit the right spots. "Shit," he yelled as he felt his body heat up. "I'm cumming...I'm...I'm fucking cumming." Banks continued to move her around in a crisscross fashion and within seconds he came so hard he sucked her nipple until it hurt.

Almost there, Bet wiggled a little more and a few seconds later she came too. Breathing heavily, they looked into each other's eyes.

"I'm gonna fall for you," she promised. "Hard."

He slapped her ass.

She grabbed the sides of his face. "Don't hurt me, Banks."

He smiled. "You safe with me."

She slowly eased up and kissed his lips. "We'll see."

The wedding chapel was small but the soldiers who lined the outside of the church and the walls inside, made it apparent that very important people were in the building.

The kings of the day, Mason and Banks sat in the front row with their girlfriends Bet and Jersey at their sides. Stretch, Banks' best soldier, was getting married and they used the event to make it apparent to the public that the Lou's and the Wales' families were officially in business, together.

For life.

Banks was dressed in black Versace pants and jacket. A gold chain rested against his shirt and his dark shades covered his mysterious eyes. Bet was something else altogether. She was wearing a white dress with gold studs that put the curves of her body on display, making it obvious to all why he chose her.

Mason went a different route. Wearing a baby blue linen suit, his wrists were dipped in diamonds and gold. His lady, Jersey, was dressed in a tight pink dress with large diamonds around her neck.

Everyone took notice of the shimmering foursome and the streets were fully aware that two kings at the height of their power were about to take over. And you were either with them or you got, got.

Brian McKnight's song, *Never Felt This Way*, played throughout the church as they watched the ceremony, Banks looked over and kissed his girl on the cheek. She smiled proudly and whispered, "You so fucking fine."

"Not finer than you." He winked and focused back on the couple.

As he thought about her he settled a few things in his mind. She wasn't Nikki but she was smart,

226   *By T. STYLES*

beautiful and went after what she wanted. He respected her ways because at least he knew where she was coming from. And he realized with her on his side they could take over the world.

He didn't want the crown before but he needed it now.

Two years passed and Banks and Mason continued to make their presence felt on the streets. Not everybody was happy. As their bank accounts increased they received a lot of pushback from rivals who weren't excited about their reunion. After some time it had got back to Banks and Mason that a new group of gangsters weren't going to sit idly by and fall under their reign.

But when Banks ordered the leaders of the organizations heads be placed on iron spikes in front of their mamas' houses as a message, the surviving members packed up and moved out of town. With no one questioning the lengths they would go to keep what they built in tact again.

Things changed and people died but the friends knew it was part of the business. Besides, they were still alive. Although there was a lot of pain and bloodshed, Banks and Mason had remained untouched because for starters they were very protected in the fort they built. Talking only to those who needed to hear their voices, they remained smart and out of the DEA's line of sight.

And because nobody knew what they went through, being both hunted and revered, their bond reached new heights. They had each other.

But it was January 10, 1995 that made Banks' world better forever.

It was the day that Bet gave birth to his first son, Spacey Wales, followed by his sons Joey, Harris and finally the love of his life, his baby girl Minnesota. Secretly named after Nikki's hometown.

Wanting to be like Banks, Mason increased his family status too with his first child Howard, then Derrick, Patterson and Arlyndo Louisville, named after his father. Mason had wanted a little girl like Banks but when he wasn't successful he decided to raise four kings instead.

The next twenty years flew by with the families getting closer than ever.

But like always, once money gets involved, nothing lasts forever.

By T. STYLES

CHAPTER TWENTY-NINE
2017

Heavy laughter filled the air.

The Lou's had been invited to dinner at the Wales' mansion which was a pastime for the families. Something they always looked forward too, especially the children. In a world that didn't understand thug millionaires, they were all they had so they remained close. And they preferred it that way.

On the right side of the beautiful long dining room table was Banks' wife Bet and his children, twenty-two-year-old Spacey, twenty-year-old Joey, eighteen-year-old Harris and his fifteen-year-old daughter Minnesota who was referred to as Minnie.

On the left side of the table were Mason and his fiancée Jersey. Along with his twenty-one year old son Howard, his nineteen-year-old son Derrick, his eighteen-year-old son Patterson and his sixteen-year-old son Arlyndo.

Collectively the two bloodlines were worth two billion easily.

After dinner was over Banks stood up and smiled at both families. "Get up, Mason!" He said grabbing his glass of champagne.

Way down on the other end, Mason rose, picked up his drink while the other hand covered his dick.

Having money didn't take the hood nigga out of him even in his forties. In fact he got more brazen, violent and belligerent as he moved through the years.

"What this family has survived no other family could imagine," Banks continued raising his glass higher. "And I couldn't have done it without my day one, Mason Lou!" The table went crazy with members clanking the sides of glasses with spoons, knives and forks.

CLANK! CLANK! CLANK!

"Alright, alright," Banks said. "Settle down."

The room grew quieter.

"Let no man try to break up what we built, less they be destroyed!" Banks yelled.

The room grew louder again upon hearing a version of their motto.

"You saying it wrong but I still love you!" Mason yelled.

"Hey, hey, hey," Banks laughed. "This my toast. Do your own."

"Yeah, pops!" Arlyndo added. "Let Unc finish."

Mason laughed. "Aight, nigga, go 'head."

"For real though," Banks grew more serious. "I couldn't have done any of this without you, my wife and both our families." He raised the glass higher. "No matter what we always have this moment! To us."

"To us!" Everyone said.

The under aged drank sparkling apple cider, the adults sipped expensive champagne.

"Now pump the music!" Banks told one of his staff members.

As Future's *Mask Off* thumped from the speakers, the youth took to the floor and danced like it was going out of style. While Banks, Mason, Bet and Jersey remained seated, looking at what they created, and believing it was good.

Arlyndo was sitting on the toilet seat in the basement bathroom of Banks' house as music blared from the speakers. Minnie was on his lap riding him like a pro. Although she loved her family, there were many secrets the spoiled brat coveted, the main one being that she was having sex with Arlyndo.

Although the two sides were close, she knew there was a line in the sand when it came to Banks. He made it clear that no daughter of his would be with a Lou despite how much he adored Mason. His reason was simple...there was no drug dealer good enough for his daughter.

"Open that pussy wider," Arlyndo said pounding into her harder. "I'm almost there."

Minnie stood up, stepped wider out and squatted on him again. "Like this, daddy?"

He gripped her waist. "Yeah, just like that." He bounced her up and down on his dick, lifting her off her feet in the process.

"Keep fucking me," she begged as her thick juices spilled down over him.

"That's what I'ma do, bitch," he continued, biting his bottom lip.

He banged into her five more times right before she hopped up and backed away. His nut splashed against the wall and over her dress as he jerked himself to completion. His frothy foam pouring out over his fingers.

"Are you crazy?" She said hitting him. "If you get me pregnant daddy would kill me! And you too!"

He laughed. "How you know I was about to bust?"

"Nigga, I know that facial expression anywhere." She hit him.

He laughed harder, got up, wiped his dick and tossed the paper in the toilet. "When you gonna tell him about us anyway?" He flushed. "All this sneaking around getting on my nerves."

"Soon, Arlyndo."

"How soon though?" He continued. "I found out from my father he trying to hook you up with one of his pilot friend's sons." He pulled his pants up and walked over to her. "Before I let that happen I'll kill both of you dead."

She grinned, loving when he talked dangerously. "Just give me some time. But I promise...that I'm not fucking with any of them green ass niggas he be trying to put me with. It's all about us."

"For life."

They kissed.

Banks walked down the steps in the basement on the hunt for Minnie. One of his aviation friends was having a party the next day and had called to confirm that his daughter would be going. But before he could tell her he noticed she was gone. Searching, when Banks walked downstairs he saw Minnie talking to Arlyndo.

Closely.

The moment his eyes landed on them he glared. "What's going on?"

They both jumped away from each other.

"Daddy, I was..."

Arlyndo said, "Sir, we want to tell—"

"Looking for Patterson and Harris," Minnie said cutting Arlyndo off. She felt he was about to let Banks know about their relationship, something she didn't want to happen.

"Is that true?" Banks asked him.

Arlyndo looked at her and back at Banks. "Uh...yeah," he said cutting his eyes at Minnie again. "I gotta go find pops though." Arlyndo walked away and up the stairs.

"What is that on your dress?" Banks asked after unknowingly touching nut and looking down at it on his thumb.

Her eyes widened. "Crème brulee."

"What's up?" He asked harsher. "With you two?"

"Daddy, nothing."

"Minnie, you can't be with him." Banks said firmly. "You know that right?"

"Ew...gross...Arlyndo is like a brother to me. Besides, I wouldn't do that. So stop playing me so close, daddy." She ran up the stairs.

He sniffed his thumb but smelled nothing.

After processing what he saw, and being unsure, Banks went looking for Mason. He loved Arlyndo like a nephew, but there was no way on the green planet he would condone her being with him. It was out of the question and he would see blood pour before he ever gave in. Not only had the Lou's gotten more reckless as the years went by, but the fact that Arlyndo was named after the man his father killed, gave him the creeps.

After searching his home for fifteen minutes, he finally found Mason alone, smoking weed outside, on his patio out back.

"Hey, what up, man," Banks said walking out, closing the sliding glass door behind him. He took the weed out of his hand and inhaled deeply.

"Did you ever think this would be us?" Mason asked looking out over Banks's pool and into the acres of land that covered his fenced in property.

Banks smiled. "What part?" He gave the weed back.

"All of it," Mason continued. "The money. Us reconnecting. All of it."

"You talk about this shit every time we get high."

"I'm serious, man." Mason glared.

Banks took a deep breath. "What's that saying you quote all the time? That I fucked up tonight?"

Mason laughed. "What God has joined together let no man tear apart..."

"Without first catching a bullet!" They both said together.

Banks laughed before quieting down. "If you ask me that says it all."

Mason nodded. "I know niggas saying you can't be in the game more than three years before the heat comes, but we have over twenty. Twenty fucking years of moving quality cocaine and I don't ever want it to end."

"We got twenty," Banks nodded. "That's true...but you know it won't last forever right?"

"Why?" Mason glared. "What's to stop us if that's what we feeling?"

"For starters I don't wanna be no drug dealer for twenty more years." He paused. "I don't want that for you either. That's why I set you up with those restaurants and them properties. So you could have a good life. A safe one."

"I thought that was just to wash my money."

"I'm fucking serious, Mason!" Banks yelled. "You gotta start thinking long term."

Mason stared at him. "You know I can't do this without you right? You know I need you and that's how we work."

"Mason..."

"I'm serious...I love this drug shit." Mason said gripping his dick. "More than anything. Even more than my own kids."

Banks shook his head and took a deep breath as he thought about what he witnessed in the basement. "I can't have our children being together."

Mason glared. "What you talking about?"

"Minnie and Arlyndo."

Mason smiled. "They not fucking with each other." He put the weed out. "They family. Like siblings."

"I'm just letting you know."

Mason looked at him closer. "Why is it that all this time, being a Lou is still a bad thing?"

"Never said that. Just can't have them together. That's where I draw the line. And nothing else need be said." He stood up, kissed the top of Mason's head and walked into the house.

After Banks and Bet received their nightly couples massage, they slipped into their matching black silk pajamas and into bed. Exhausted, Banks eased behind his wife and kissed the back of her neck.

A knock on the door broke them out of the comfort zone they were about to fall into. "Come in," Banks yelled.

Stretch walked inside wearing a grey suit. As Banks' personal muscle, he never left his side. Both him and his wife lived in the mansion to ensure the family was safe at all times. "Everyone's asleep, boss." He looked at Bet and back at Banks. "Need anything else?"

"I'm good." He paused. "Just lock up."

Stretch nodded and walked out.

Banks took a deep breath and grabbed his wife tighter. "I think Minnie may be seeing Arlyndo."

"Okay...what you want to do about it?"

"They can't be together."

"Exactly." Bet paused. "Besides, Arlyndo has gotten arrested five times this year alone. The last person we want her with in the world is him."

"I'm praying things haven't gone further than we can stop." Banks paused. "I mean...have you seen anything? Or did she say anything to you when you took her to the nail salon today?"

"If she had you know I would've told you already." She sighed. "But between brokering the real estate deals and the restaurants, I haven't seen much of anything. I'm sorry."

Banks nodded. "Have you gotten managers to take over like I asked?"

She turned around and faced him. "Why, Banks?"

He glared. "What you mean why?"

"I love being able to start businesses and see them grow. Why you want me to stop now?"

"Remember our agreement over twenty years ago?"

"No, Banks, do *you* remember?" She asked. "I promised to take care of you. And to love you. And to give you children." She kissed his lips. "I've done that. But you haven't lived up to your part of the deal."

"How you figure?"

"The secret meetings. The getting off the phone when I come into a room."

"I'm not cheating." He said confidently. "You know me better than that."

"I know you not sleeping around," she paused. "I don't wanna have to kill a bitch out here."

He laughed. "Bet, cut that shit out."

"I'm talking about the secrecy, Banks," she continued. "You promised you'd always be real. But the only thing you seem to care about lately is flying and meeting with strangers I don't know."

"Soon all will be revealed." He kissed her nose. "Trust me."

"I trust nobody more."

"Good." He paused. "Then find people to run your businesses. And keep an eye out for Minnie and Arlyndo. If those two get together it could revisit evil places our family never wants to go."

"I will."

"I'm serious...I don't play when it comes to my daughter. Then again you know that already."

CHAPTER THIRTY

Spacey Wales and Howard Louisville were playing pool in the basement of the Wales' mansion. Howard was shirtless, and the designer jeans he wore dragged downward, revealing his white boxers. Spacey on the other hand was more put together, with his skinny designer jeans and plain white t-shirt.

After Spacey called his pocket, and made the shot, Howard tossed down the stick in rage. "You cheating ass, nigga." He pointed in his face.

Spacey rolled his eyes. "That's why I don't like to play with you." Spacey sat his pool stick on the table and racked the balls. A job that was supposed to be Howard's since he took an 'L'. "You get too mad."

"It ain't about getting mad, it's about you cheating."

"You wanna play again or not?" Spacey asked with an attitude.

"Fuck you say?" Howard said walking up to him, injecting fear into Spacey's beating heart.

"Nothing, Howard."

"Then shut the fuck up about all that other shit before I drop you." He pointed in his face. "I ain't—"

"Get out that nigga's grill," Derrick Louisville said walking down the steps with his brother Patterson. He scratched his baldhead. "Every time I turn around you in his face. I don't even see why he deals with you."

By T. STYLES

"Always trying to punk a nigga and shit," Patterson added. His long neat dreads hanging over his shoulders.

"If this nigga stop cheating," Howard said grabbing his stick. "I wouldn't have to get in his shit."

Spacey waved him off but for real his heart was twerking. He loved the Lou's like brothers but when it came to their mood swings, especially Howard's, it always put him on edge. He couldn't count the number of times Howard jumped on him in rage, resulting in Spacey losing each time. Spacey would never tell Banks, as much as he wanted, fearing he would look bad to the Lou's and his own father.

"I gotta go to the bathroom," Spacey said.

"Well hurry the fuck up so I can get my win back," Howard said.

Spacey shook his head and pulled the bathroom door open. His heart dropped when he saw his sister Minnie's bare ass on the sink, while Arlyndo was on his knees eating her out.

"What the fuck?" Spacey said with wide eyes. "What ya'll doing?"

Arlyndo stood up and wiped his lips with the back of his hand, before taking a deep swallow to clear his cum filled mouth.

Minnie jumped off the sink, pulled down her dress and pulled up her panties.

The Lou brothers laughed when they realized what was going on. "That nigga in there eating ass!" Howard laughed pointing his finger at Arlyndo.

"No I wasn't!" Arlyndo yelled, pushing out the bathroom with Minnie following closely like a shadow.

"I know what we saw, nigga!" Patterson added, following him.

"I'm telling dad," Spacey yelled. "He gonna flip when he find this shit out, Minnie." He said to his sister.

The entire room froze.

Everyone in attendance knew what his threat meant. If Banks ever learned that they were together not only was the relationship over, the Lou's would lose access to the best cocaine in the United States of Fucking America. Which would mean extreme changes to their lifestyle. Changes the fellas weren't willing to make.

Ever.

Howard, Derrick and Patterson crowded around him.

"Nah, you ain't gonna do that," Howard said pointing a stiff finger into his chest.

"Why...why ya'll getting in my face?" Spacey asked while trembling. "I...I—"

"Because that ain't what brothers do to each other," Derrick said to him. "Now go upstairs, I wanna talk to Arlyndo and Minnie. But keep your mouth closed, Spacey. I ain't fucking around."

Spacey looked at his sister and the Lou's, before walking up the steps with his head hung low like he'd been the one caught eating ass.

"Ya'll bounce too," Derrick said to his brothers.

"Ain't nobody listening to you, college boy," Howard snapped.

"Get the fuck upstairs before I go off!" Derrick said louder.

Howard may have been older and scarier, but Derrick's name rang bells on the streets. Even with being a college student at the University Of Maryland, he was capable of many dark things.

Slowly the brothers crawled up the stairs, leaving the trio alone.

"Fuck is wrong with you, lil' nigga?" Derrick snapped on Arlyndo.

"I was just—"

"Playing your bitch like a ho."

Minnie looked down at her wiggly toes. "I didn't mind" She blushed. "It feels good when he eats me out."

"I wasn't eating you out!" He lied.

"Nigga, shut yo bitch ass up!" Derrick wiped his hand down his face and tried to calm down. "Whatever this is...it's gotta end." He pointed at both of them. "We ain't 'bout to be short in the pockets 'cause you can't keep your dick out the boss's daughter." He paused. "Okay?"

Silence.

"Are you listening?" Derrick said louder.

Arlyndo looked at Minnie, grabbed her hand and walked up the steps.

Leaving Derrick alone.

Mason had a long day...

Flopping on the sofa, he dragged his hands down his face as he breathed heavily into his palms. Banks talking about leaving the lifestyle had his mind twirling and the fact that he didn't want forever in the dope game, complexed his little thug heart.

"Slave," Mason yelled.

A minute later Jersey came out from the back wearing high heels and a dog collar, which dragged a thick link chain.

"On your knees."

She smiled and lowered her height before crawling over to him.

Loving the power, he looked down at her, removed his dick and stroked it to a thickness, before placing himself into her mouth.

By T. STYLES

Leaning his head back, within a few minutes, all his problems went away.

CHAPTER THIRTY-ONE

Banks and Spacey were flying in the air as Banks piloted his plane he called *The Wales*. With over twenty years of aviation experience under his belt, the man knew the skies like dope boys knew their blocks. When Banks was on his plane nothing else mattered and he felt one with God. And there was nothing better than sharing it with his family but unfortunately Spacey was the only one who truly appreciated his craft.

Things weren't all good with them however.

When it came to the boys it was believed that Banks was harder on them, choosing instead to pour his love into the only daughter of the family, Minnie. While some acted as if they didn't care, it was a constant battle for Spacey, and he would give anything to take Minnie's place in Banks' heart. Since begging for his attention by asking to go any and everywhere with him didn't work, he decided to try something else.

Straight snitching.

"Dad...can I ask you something?"

Banks nodded as he continued to pilot.

"Do you love me?"

Banks looked over at him and frowned. "Why would you ask me something like that?" He pressed a few keys on his control panel.

By T. STYLES

"When I told you I wanted to work closer with you on the streets, you said no." He shrugged. "But when my brothers asked you let them."

"Because the streets aren't you, son." He looked over at him. "You know that."

"But they *are* me!" He said a little louder. "If you just give me a chance."

"That's not happening," Banks said.

Spacey took a deep breath and looked down. "But why?"

Banks sighed. "Just because you ain't no drug dealer like Joey and Harris, don't mean you don't have purpose." He paused. "To be honest I'm glad the streets ain't in you."

Spacey's eyebrows rose. "Really?"

"Yes." Banks nodded. "I wish it wasn't in me either. But my father pushed me to this shit a long time ago." He paused. "But trust me, ain't no long term future in coke."

"But we have a life with money and—"

"That could be taken away at any moment." He paused. "Think about it. Not many drug dealers make twenty years in the game. Even my luck won't last forever."

Spacey nodded. "I have something else to tell you." He paused. "And I know you don't wanna hear this but you always saying we can't have no secrets between each other."

Banks glared. "What is it?"

"Are you gonna promise not to get mad?" Spacey continued. "Because I don't want to tell you if—"

"You know I don't make promises I can't keep."

Spacey sighed.

"What is it, son?"

"I think...well...I caught Minnie and Arlyndo together."

Banks frowned. "What exactly does that mean?"

"He was eating her out in the bathroom."

Suddenly the plane dropped.

"Dad, what's happening?" Spacey asked as his heart rocked in his chest.

Banks was doing his best to maintain control of the aircraft but after hearing the news, and making such a sudden move with the controls, it was hard to regain authority.

It was obvious they were about to crash.

CHAPTER THIRTY-TWO

Linden sat in his small house watching reruns of Family Feud when there was a knock at the door. Instead of being more cautious, he opened it without asking who was on the other side. Besides, he had a repeat visitor month after month, year after year so there was really no surprise.

When it was ajar, Stretch walked through the door and looked down at Linden who sat back down on the small decrepit brown sofa. He was in charge of this job, which irritated him to no end. "You again, huh?" Linden asked scratching his salt and pepper beard.

Stretch smirked. "I'm just the delivery boy." He reached into his pocket and pulled out a thick folded manila envelope filled with fifty thousand dollars.

Linden shook his head. "You know the routine. Just throw it over there." He nodded toward a brown wicker basket with twenty envelopes just like it inside.

"Why you doing this to yourself?" Stretch tossed the envelope on the stack. It made a small thud. "Don't you get tired of it all?"

"What you talking about?"

"You have almost half a million over there...in cash." He paused and looked around at the small dump. "Yet you moved out of your crib in Baltimore and set up here. Why?"

"I don't want Wales money. Ain't got no use for it."

"So you prefer to live like a bum?"

"Nah...the real question is why would my little brother turn his back on his own family for a Wales nigga?" He paused. "The one person responsible for killing his own father? Can you answer me that?"

Stretch shrugged. "That shit was before my time."

"Is that right?" He smiled, showing his yellowing teeth. Linden was never the best looking nigga in a lineup but with time he had gotten worse. And more bitter. "The reason I'm asking you is because you and that nigga Banks look just like brothers." He laughed. "Then again you've heard that before."

It was true. Stretch had heard those words before. Instead of humoring him he rolled his eyes. "All I'm saying is you should take the money Mason be blessing you with and buy another place to stay." He walked toward the door. "It smells like six bags of wet shit in here."

When Stretch left, Mason stood up and walked into the back room where a friend of his sat on the edge of the bed eating a bowl of Cap'n Crunch Berries cereal. He was a large man who was so tall they ditched his real name of Clyde and called him Tops instead. A career criminal since birth, he had just gotten home two days ago and was looking to get into more trouble.

"You still willing to put in that work?" Linden asked leaning on the doorframe.

Tops put the bowl down on the bed. "So you really gonna kill your own brother?" He asked with a jaw full of colorful cereal.

"I ain't got no brother. Now you wanna make money or not?"

Tops picked up his bowl and shrugged. "If you don't give a fuck why should I?" He shoved a shitload of cereal into his mouth. "Just let me know when you wanna do it."

The smell of urine and mold was in the air.

Banks stood in front of Garret who had been hitting his phone repeatedly non-stop, calling it urgent. They were in one of the Wales' many decrepit real estate properties that he was going to fix up. In the past Banks would've never exposed himself by meeting with a low level. Besides, Garret was one of Mason's customers, so he didn't understand why he was calling him anyway. Or why he showed up. But for some reason Banks was intrigued.

Also in attendance were Banks' sons, Joey and Harris who stood behind him ready to protect him at all cost.

To be honest after almost crashing his plane, upon hearing what was happening between his baby girl and Arlyndo, the last thing he wanted was to talk to the reckless nigga who didn't understand chain of command standing before him.

But there he stood, ready to provide a listening ear.

For the moment anyway.

"What that got to do with us?" Joey asked Garret. The shorter of the sons, Joey still possessed the smooth light skin of his father and siblings. He was also as mean as a rattlesnake if you caught him in a bad way.

"I know it's wrong but last night Mason killed three of my men."

"Why?" Joey asked.

"Because he extended them a pack when I was on vacation and they were three dollars short on the pay back." He said excitedly. "Three dollars short." He held up three fingers as if folks couldn't count. "The nigga's crazy."

"And you gotta take that up with Unc!" Harris shrugged. He was known for cooking coke and his muscular physique whenever he walked into a room. "This not Wales business."

"That's fucked up though," Garret continued throwing up his arms. "I bring you big business, Banks." He pointed at him. "Even if it is through Mason. And this is how you—"

"You foul," Banks interjected. "And I don't deal with foul niggas."

"So you rather not have my money then to sell to me on the side?" He glared.

Seeing Garret's sinister look, Joey and Harris covered their father. "Because of the business you brought I'll let you live...but you cut off supply."

Garret wanted to shit in the seat of his jeans. "So now I can't get no work at all?"

"You dry out here..." Banks snapped. "And if you hit my number again you dead too." Banks said firmly, before walking out. His sons following behind him.

"We'll see about that," Garret said with rage in his eyes.

CHAPTER THIRTY-THREE

Mason walked up and down the aisles looking at the cakes of crack cocaine lining the tables in one of his many trap houses. Outside of his artwork, which now gained him a huge underground following, moving dope was the love of his life. He smiled when he thought about his operation and how smoothly he was able to shake niggas off his trail.

Every time the cops or a hitter tried to bring him down, he would relocate his operation before they made a move. As a result nothing outsiders tried to do to him would work.

He was untouchable.

When his stomach started to growl, he walked upstairs to grab something to eat. Music blasted from a radio speaker as he moved over to a flimsy card table, which was layered with boxes of hot Chinese food in the living room. His sons Howard, Derrick and Patterson were seated on the sofa eating. While Arlyndo sat at the table with Minnie on his lap enjoying his meal.

Mason turned the radio off and smiled at the young couple with pride.

Unlike his best friend, he saw their union as hope for the future. And he was confident that in time he would be able to convince his friend of the same.

By T. STYLES

"I heard about the other night, Arlyndo." Mason said, grabbing a box of shrimp fried rice and eating straight out of it with his fingertips. Despite dustings of coke being on his nails. "You have to be careful."

"I didn't think nobody was gonna walk in that bathroom," he said as Minnie fed him a shrimp egg roll dipped in hot mustard sauce. "Definitely not a Wales."

"But that's just it," Derrick injected. He had been mad ever since he found out about them. "You not thinking."

"Nigga, shut the fuck up," Arlyndo said, showing off for Minnie. "Always in my business and shit."

By the time Derrick had smacked him upside the head Arlyndo was too embarrassed to say anything.

"Cut all that shit out," Mason laughed, thinking the rough housing between his sons was masculine. "Shit will work out for the Lou's. It always does."

Arlyndo, a big brat, got up and ran to the bathroom in embarrassment.

Minnie followed him.

Seeing how upset his youngest boy was, Mason walked to the bathroom door and knocked on it with a hard fist. "Stop all that whining! He was just fucking with you."

"Leave me alone!" Arlyndo yelled from behind the door. "I hate him! I hate everybody!"

Mason laughed, flopped down at the table and continued to eat. "That young girl got him going crazy."

"Dad, you gotta put an end to that shit." He paused. "He gonna ruin everything. I feel it in my heart."

Mason sat the box on the table. "Listen, I know you worried, Derrick."

"Me too, pops," Howard said. "I got a bad feeling about this."

"Since when do you two agree with each other?" Mason frowned.

"I'm not with it either," Patterson added. "I mean...since we making a list. I think it's disloyal to Unc for you to let them be together when he doesn't want it that way."

Mason looked at his sons and folded his arms over his chest. "Like I said, ain't nothing to be worried about. Banks talking shit but when he realizes you can't pull them apart he'll change." He ran his hand down his face. "If you ask me they're the hope for the Lou and Wales' future."

Derrick sighed. "But if Banks finds out everything we built gone." He paused. "Please dad...stop this shit now. I'm begging—"

"Stop worrying."

KNOCK. KNOCK. KNOCK.

Everyone reached for their hammers on their hips when they heard banging at the front door. In investigation mode, Howard got up and slowly walked to the door. Looking out the peephole his eyes widened when he saw who was on the other side. "It's Banks."

Mason stood up. "Let him in."

"Are you serious?" Derrick whispered. "Minnie in here." He pointed at the bathroom door.

Mason crossed his arms over his chest. "Let him in. My car out front. He knows I'm here."

Howard shook his head and unlocked the door. Banks walked in, a look of seriousness on his face.

"Hey, Unc," Howard said.

Banks dapped each of Mason's spawn.

"I'm about to go to the house, Pops," Derrick said looking at the bathroom door and back at Mason. "Jersey cooking my favorite tonight."

"Well save some for me," Mason said.

Howard, Derrick and Patterson exited also, leaving the two alone in the living room.

Banks flopped on the sofa and ran his hands down his face.

"Niggas ate already and eating again." Mason paused. "Greedy ass kids." He took a deep breath. "You aight, man?"

"I had a long night." Banks sighed. "What can I say?"

"Heard you almost crashed too," Mason said as he stood up and walked over to him. "I keep telling you black people not meant to be in the sky."

"Well that's where I'm most like myself." He paused. "But look...I gotta talk to you about something."

Mason looked back at the bathroom door and then Banks. "Wanna talk outside?"

"Nah...we can rap in here." He sighed and clasped his hands together. "I won't be long."

Mason nodded. "Speak."

"Garrett reached out."

Mason sat next to him. "For fucking what?"

"Said he wanted to buy straight from me instead of you." He paused. "How this nigga even get my number?"

"I don't know...I...I..." Mason's face crawled into an evil glare. He couldn't wait to lay hands on him after his reckless move for going to Banks behind his back. "I think when we first got in business I might've given it to him...I can't remember." He scratched his scalp.

"Well like I said he reached out." He shook his head. "The fact that he thought that little cash he be handing down the pipeline is life changing for niggas like us is beyond me."

Mason jumped up and slammed his fist into his palm. "That nigga dead."

Banks looked up at him. "I told him he cut off too."

"Good!" Mason continued pacing the floor. "The nerve of that dude. No loyalty at all."

"Exactly." Banks paused and looked at him intensely. "Speaking of loyalty, there's something else I want to talk to you about. I think Arlyndo and Minnie may be seeing each other. Sexually. If that's true I need that to stop. And I'ma need your help too."

Mason frowned. "Why?"

"We talked about this already, man." Banks said. "Why you making me repeat myself? They kids and can't be together."

Mason shrugged. "You told me how you wanted things to be and I—"

"Minnie only fifteen and I don't want her having sex." Banks said firmly. "She just a kid. And Arlyndo is too."

"Who said they were having—"

"I don't give a fuck what they doing to be honest," Banks said louder. "I don't want 'em together!" Banks repeated. "Do you understand? Ain't nothing you can do to get me to change my mind."

Mason shook his head. "Whoa."

Banks got up and walked toward the door. Feeling bad he took a deep breath. "Look, man, I ain't mean to come at you like—"

"You meant to come at me just like that," Mason responded. "Like we ain't got a past. Like I don't know all your fucking secrets."

"Is that a threat?" Banks glared.

Silence.

Banks' mind was made up and there was nothing else that could be said. Minnie would never be with his son on his watch. He grabbed the doorknob to leave and then looked at the bathroom. "I gotta piss right quick." He moved toward it and Mason blocked him.

"The toilet not working."

Banks walked around him. "I gotta piss. I'll pour some water in..." When Banks opened the door, and saw his daughter hiding in the dark with Arlyndo, his blood boiled and his light skin reddened. Slowly he rotated his head toward Mason. "You knew my daughter was in here and ain't tell me?"

"Come on, man," Mason said throwing up his hands. "They in love."

"Minnie, go get in my car," Banks said, nostrils flaring, eyes still on his friend.

Minnie said, "But I—"

"GET THE FUCK IN MY CAR!"

"I hate you daddy!" She stormed out of the bathroom and exited the house, crying.

Arlyndo walked up to Banks. "Sir, I know you don't want me with your daughter but I want to tell you, I love her so much."

Banks ignored him, eyes still on his father.

Pointing in Mason's face, taking a deep breath Banks walked out the door.

CHAPTER THIRTY-FOUR

Fresh air rolled into the open window in the Owner's Suite at the Lou Mansion. Trying to relax, Mason lie on the bed looking into darkness, until Jersey rubbed his back softly. "Are you okay, Master?" She asked. "You've been uptight for hours. Did something happen at the trap?"

Mason thought about the way Banks left, and the look of disappointment in his eyes. His mind was rolling with thoughts on what would happen if seeing their kids together really did fuck with business. And yet he didn't want to talk about it because his sons warned him and he didn't listen.

"Why you still here?" He responded. "After all these years?"

She leaned over, cut her lamp on and sat up in bed. Her back against the headboard. "What you mean?"

He sat next to her. "You over forty and for real you let yourself go a bit." He paused. "And you starting to gross me out too."

"Mason, I—"

"Nothing about you makes my dick hard anymore." He continued, doing his best to make her feel the pain he was in at the moment. "You can't even fuck without complaining about your knees." He paused. "The only reason you still here is because you gave me four sons.

WAR   261

But for that you wouldn't even be in my house right now."

She touched his arm and he jumped out of bed. "I'm gonna go see about our son."

"Mason, I—"

He walked out and slammed the door.

Trudging down the hallway, he moved toward Arlyndo's room. Pulling the door open, he saw his youngest child on the floor in a fetal position crying his eyes out. Although he should've been more disgusted, his heart broke for his spawn. After all, it had been two weeks and he hadn't heard from the love of his life.

The boy was severely broken.

Still, the misery Arlyndo felt had to give at some point.

"Son," Mason said softly closing the door behind himself. "You can't be like this forever."

"But he won't...he won't let her call me." He sniffled.

Mason sat on the edge of the bed and sighed. "Then what you gonna do about it?" Mason continued. "Sit over there like a bitch and cry your eyes out?"

"I don't know what to—"

"If you want your girl back fight for her!" Mason continued. "But the crying stops today." He pointed at the floor. "Otherwise I want you out my house because

I can't take this shit no more." Mason walked toward the door, slamming it behind him.

He moved downstairs and picked up his cell phone that sat on the kitchen counter. Taking a deep breath he dialed a number and waited. "Banks, we almost dry out here on the streets, man. You gotta hit me back. Tell me something. You owe me that much."

CHAPTER THIRTY-FIVE

When a tall white man carrying a large brown expandable pocket folder walked up to the front door of the Wales Mansion, Banks opened it, handed him a suitcase and closed the door. The moment he turned around, before he could examine the contents he saw Bet standing in front of him with her arms crossed over her body.

"What's going on, Banks?" She paused. "Who was that man?"

"I'll tell you when—"

"Tell me now!" She said louder, one of her hands clenched into a fist. "I'm tired of waiting on the right fucking time!"

Banks looked around, grabbed her hand and yanked her into his office. "What I tell you about the disrespect and raising your voice to me?" He paused. "I'm not one of the kids."

She took a deep breath. "I'm sorry it's just that..." She paused. "I can't wait anymore for you to tell me what you doing. I need to know now. If I'm your partner you can't hold me in the dark any longer. Please, baby."

Banks took a deep breath, locked the door and flopped into his black plush leather desk chair. "Sit."

She took a seat, her thick legs crossed like her arms.

By T. STYLES

"We're leaving."

Her arms dropped at her sides. "We're leaving? What are you—"

"For the past twenty years, I've been, I've been working on our way out."

"Banks, I'm not understanding."

"You understand," he said softly. "You understand clearly. I made you my wife because I knew you were smart not because it was love at first sight. Right now you just not listening."

"Where can we move that Nidia wouldn't find us? Where can we move where Mason wouldn't find us? You don't just pick up and leave because you don't like the game no more."

"Why not?" Banks yelled. "Give me one scenario that ends with us walking out of here with our boys and daughter alive? Or not in jail?" He paused. "I don't want that for our family."

"I get that but...where can we go?" She sighed. "Huh? This is dangerous, Banks. You should've talked to me about this first."

He smiled, stood up and grabbed the folder the stranger brought earlier. Thumbing through it he removed a photo showcasing a vivid body of water. In the center of it was an island." He pointed to it. "We're moving there."

Her eyes widened and she removed it from his hand. "What is this?" She looked up at him.

"Wales Island."

Her jaw dropped. "Are you saying you...you..."

"Bought us a way out." He pulled up one of the chairs and sat next to her. "It's not empty either, Bet. Our home is built. Our new cars are there. We have a staff. We have islanders, a family who has dedicated their lives to making things right on our land. The only thing they're waiting on is us."

"But..."

"I know you're scared," he continued grabbing both of her hands. "That's part of the reason I didn't bring it to you before. Moving is scary but if you love me, if you love our family, you know we have no choice. We can't survive another twenty years of dealing cocaine."

"If you love *me* why would you do something so permanent without telling me?"

"I did it *because* I love you." He grabbed her hand. "Don't you see? I don't wanna be like one of them niggas in prison, doing a bid because they didn't snitch. Because you know that would be me too. Doing other people's time because I'm staying true to the vows of the street." He kissed her cheek. "I wanna live out the rest of my life without worrying about your safety or the safety of our kids."

"Banks...I..." Unable to finish her sentence, she started crying. "I'm sorry but I'm so confused."

"It's okay." He grabbed her hand and she sat in his lap. "Listen, I would never do anything so drastic without thinking things through. And I know when we leave it's gonna be foul but I'm gonna do my best to make sure Mason good. But if Nidia still doesn't wanna fuck with him directly after all these years, we still out of here."

"The kids?"

"They gonna be mad at first until they see this place. It's beautiful."

"Minnie's gonna lose it. Especially if she in love with that boy."

"Yeah, well she doesn't have a choice."

"But are you gonna come clean?" She touched his face and looked into his eyes. "About *everything*?"

"Are you talking about that?"

"Yes, Banks." She paused. "You can't tell them this is their new life without telling them everything."

"I'll reveal all once we're there." He paused. "For now I want my family away from here. We can't waste anymore time. Stretch going with us too. And his wife."

"Wow, Banks." She paused. "For the first time in my life I don't know how this will end."

"What part?"

She picked up the picture. "What if your dream wasn't thought all the way through? I mean, you have a way of checking off every box but what if you missed something?"

"I didn't." He said squeezing her hand. "I can even fly us there. I been working on this plan for over twenty years. Every detail. Wrote about it everyday in my composition books. It's time."

She sniffled. "So that's what they were for?"

"Trust me...this will work. I see it in my mind!"

By T. STYLES

CHAPTER THIRTY-SIX

Linden sat in a car across the street from the Lou's mansion. Tops was in the passenger seat next to him, also looking at the multi-million dollar home with envy. "Wow...Mason really did come up," Linden said focusing on the iron gate.

"So what you want me to do about your nephews?"

"I don't want 'em hit," Linden said looking at him, and then the house. "If they with him don't shoot. Unless you have a clear shot of Mason."

Tops nodded. "I talked to a friend of mine." He paused. "Mason is hosting some art show for his recent paintings." He looked at Linden. "But...is it true?"

"Yep." Linden nodded. "Everything you heard."

"So this nigga actually kills people and uses their blood to—"

"Are you sure you gonna be able to do the job?" Linden said cutting him off.

"I'm broke, man," he paused. "This gonna put me back where I need to be so I don't have to beg and kill these niggas out here no more." He paused. It was good Linden came to him because he was going to hit him over the head and take the envelopes of money. But Linden had hidden them, foiling his future attempt. "So yes...I can do the job."

"Good, but I want it clean. A shot to the head. I don't want him suffering. He still my baby brother."

Tops nodded. "Consider it done."

Banks and his family ate quietly around the table in the dining room. Since it was only the Wales, the table extenders were removed so that the family was able to sit closer. It was supposed to be a good night and their chef made delicious gumbo with rice and fresh cornbread, a Wales favorite.

When the dessert was served, chocolate cake, Banks took a deep breath and grabbed his wife's hand. "I have to talk to you all about something." He paused. "Very important."

Everyone looked at one another and put their forks down. They clanked against the plates as they dropped. All had smiles on their faces.

Minnie on the other hand, rolled her eyes. After being followed by security guards seventeen hours a day, except when sleep, she wasn't able to talk to Arlyndo. And this made her hate her father even more.

"What is it, dad?" Spacey asked.

"We're moving."

The moment he heard those words Spacey smiled wider. He didn't like living in Maryland anyway, around the Lou's, so anyplace new was a breath of fresh air. "Love it!"

"Where we going?" Joey frowned.

"I bought our own island."

Bet squeezed Banks' hand softly. "It's beautiful," she said. "I saw the layout and—"

"So I'm supposed to leave my boyfriend?" Minnie asked. "And move with ya'll to some foreign fucking country?"

"You don't have a boyfriend." Banks said calmly. "I done told you that already."

"YES I DO!" She yelled standing up. "You just don't wanna see me happy!" She continued. "You don't know what it means to be in love with somebody and not be able to see them. You're ruining my fucking life."

Banks thought about Nikki. "Minnie, you have no idea what I know."

Bet released Banks hand, knowing he was having a *'Nikki Moment'* again.

"I don't wanna move!" Minnie continued. "I mean, what is it, daddy? You wanna fuck me or something? You want me all to yourself so you don't got to share no more? Is that it?"

Upon hearing her daughter's foul mouth, Bet stood up, walked around the table and slapped her straight.

"I FUCKING HATE YOU, UGLY BITCH!" She ran out of the room crying. "I HATE EVERYBODY!"

"I'll talk to her," Joey said, getting up to leave the table.

"I know this is hard," Banks continued talking to the rest of the family. "I do. But we have to make this move now if we want to get out of this game alive."

"But when did you decide to do all this?" Harris asked. "And why didn't you tell us sooner? I have friends...and people I wanna say goodbye too."

"I wanted to make sure things were going as planned first. And now they are."

"What about Mason?" Harris asked. "He'll never let you walk away."

"He doesn't have a choice." Banks said firmly. "And I have some things in the works for him that might make things a little smoother." He took a deep breath. "In the meantime this must stay between us." He paused. "Don't tell anybody. Not your girlfriends. Not your teachers. No one."

Silence.

"I can stay quiet," Harris said. "But what about Minnie?"

CHAPTER THIRTY-SEVEN

Mason sped down the highway with a bottle of vodka in hand. When he finally got to the location he was going, he pressed a code and the wrought iron gate with the words THE WALES spread across the front opened, allowing him access. Once in the driveway, he grabbed the bottle, left his car door open and banged on the front door.

Within minutes Bet appeared on the other side with a smile on her face. "Mason."

"Where is he?" Mason continued.

Suddenly a few soldiers surrounded Mason, eager to throw him out.

"I have it," she told them. "Please leave."

They looked at Mason again and walked away.

"Come inside." She opened the door wider.

Mason stumbled inside, his body swerving. "Where is he, Bet?"

"Are you hungry?"

"Bet, I love you but I'ma need you to stop fucking with me right now." He said pointing at the floor. "Now where the fuck is Banks? He messing with my money since he ain't making deliveries and I'ma need that to stop. Today!"

She placed a hand on his shoulder and walked him toward her office. Unlike the dark chocolate colors of Banks' space, Bet's office was gold and burgundy and was fit for a queen. "Sit on the sofa." She pointed at it. "I'll be right back."

Mason flopped down into the plushness and poured more liquor in his mouth. When it was gone, he sat the bottle down and ran two hands down his face. He was agitated by it all. The fact that he didn't think smarter with handling Arlyndo and Minnie. The fact that Banks didn't want the kids together, even though he thought it was a good idea. And the fact that once again their friendship was in jeopardy.

This time forever.

A few minutes later Spacey, Joey and Harris walked inside Bet's office.

Each hugged Mason and said, "Hey, Unc", as they watched his every move.

"Where is your fa...your..." Mason tried to complete his sentence but was short when he burped a gaseous bubble of alcohol. "Your father?"

"He's in the air," Spacey said. "Flying. You okay?"

"I will be if I can get back up." He pointed to the bottle. "Kinda...kinda had too much to drink."

They nodded.

"I'm gonna see what ma doing," Joey said before walking off. Seeing Mason in a bad way broke his heart because he fucked with him hard.

Ready to get on everybody's nerves, and wearing a long man's white t-shirt, Minnie appeared in the doorway. "How is he?" Tears ran down her face as she awaited his answer.

"Other than missing you?"

She nodded, and wiped tears away roughly. "Can you tell him if I could I would—"

"As much as I wanted to see you both together...it's...it's really over, kid." He paused. "And I'm really sorry about that but—"

She ran out screaming and crying.

Seconds later Bet appeared holding two black duffels. Walking up to him she threw them on the sofa. "Is this enough?"

His eyes widened.

He stood up. Opening each, he saw kilos upon kilos of uncooked white. "This a lot."

"You can move it right?"

He nodded with a huge smile on his face. "Yeah but...I mean...its gonna take a minute to get the bread up. I'm not liquid right—"

"We know you good for it, Mason."

Although he felt somewhat relieved that he was back in business, he was still irritated that he hadn't spoken to his closest comrade. Yes it was about the money. But when it came to him and Banks it was about so much more. They held secrets that not a lot of people knew about, which is why Banks ignoring him fucked with his mind.

Hard.

Minnie appeared back in the doorway. One for the dramatics, she often ran off into the house only to return when no one was checking for her.

"Why he not taking my calls?" Mason asked Bet. "This not like Banks."

Minnie stepped up ready to tell it all. "He's not taking your call because—"

Knowing what she was about to say, Spacey and Harris rushed toward Minnie like an open quarterback before she finished her sentence. With Spacey's hand firmly against her lips, they shoved her out before she could speak on things that they were sure were bound to set the Lou's and the Wales' back five generations.

"What was she about to say?" He asked Bet.

She moved closer. "Family matters."

"Family matters huh?"

She nodded. "Listen, Mason, give Banks some time. Because what I know about him is this...he loves you. Like a brother." She paused. "But he was hurt about Minnie and Arlyndo. And I am too if I'm being honest."

He nodded. "I know...and if he gives me a chance to...I mean...just have him call me. I really am sorry about the kids...I just...I'm sorry."

She hugged him and kissed the side of his face. "Go home, Mason."

He nodded and grabbed the bags. Tossing them over each shoulder he walked out.

CHAPTER THIRTY-EIGHT

After Banks flew his plane to Texas, he sat with Nidia on her patio, trying to convince her of something he knew would never fly. "I appreciate the meal," Banks said wiping his mouth with an expensive linen cloth.

"What is your type?" She asked as she continued to work on her lobster and corn bisque by a patio fireplace. "In a woman?"

Banks laughed. "You met Bet before remember?"

She nodded. "I do." She shrugged. "Very pretty, don't get me wrong, but you two act more like business partners than lovers."

He sighed. "She's perfect. Knows what I need before I ask. Takes care of her body. Our family." He shrugged. "I mean, what more can I say?"

"You had another...when you were much younger." She paused. "What was her name?"

Banks' temples started to throb just remembering the past. Talking about Nikki was a sore topic, even to that day. "What is this about, Nidia?"

"Why is it that you never fucked me?"

Banks laughed. "We talking about this again?"

Still beautiful, even with age, she wiped her long black and grey hair out of her face. "Well, Banks, it's not often that I'm rejected. So I'm intrigued."

"I get that." He smiled placing lobster shells in a silver bucket. "But for me, it's about so much more." He wiped his mouth with the napkin again, tossing it on the table.

"I know."

"You know?" He repeated.

"I do," She said giving him a serious look. One that said she was more knowledgeable than she let on. "Now that we've gotten that out the way, what brings you here?"

"I have five hundred million under the floorboards in my plane."

"I know that too."

He looked at the acres of land where his plane sat and squinted. Now that he observed he saw men going through it in a distance with flashlights. "Wait...they grabbed the cash already?" He frowned.

"Had to make sure you weren't wired up, or had some bomb attached to your aircraft." She shrugged. "You know, one of the reasons I prefer to discuss business in the bedroom is because I can make sure I'm not being recorded. We were going to check your body next but you never take me up on my invitation."

He smiled. "Is that right?"

"I know you're loyal." She licked her fingers seductively. "But what I don't understand is what you brought the money to my home for?"

"I want out."

By T. STYLES

She sighed. "I always knew that with you, this day would come." She paused. "Always thought it would be sooner."

"I'm sorry. It's just that I don't see a future in this forever."

"Why should I let a man who has given me more wealth and less problems then I ever had get away?"

"Because it's just that." He paused. "I've made you wealthy. Now I want to be free."

"Wealthier. I was already a billionaire a few times over."

"Nidia, it's time to let me and my family go. Please. And I'm hoping the extra half a billion would make you see things my way."

She looked at him for a long time. As if studying every inch of his face. Suddenly she sighed. "Okay."

His eyes widened. "Okay?"

"I'm gonna take the money and let you go."

"Really?"

"I like you, Banks. And because I know cocaine is in your blood, I feel confident that you'll come back to me. So if I kill you, like I'm capable of doing, I'm going against what I know in my heart to be true."

"I need to be straight...this is it for me." He said seriously.

"You don't divorce Cocaine. She divorces you. You'll return."

Banks smiled although he was certain he was never coming back, no matter what she was talking about. "There's one other thing."

She crossed her legs and grabbed her red wine. "No."

"But he's so much different now."

"Since when have you known me to go back on my word?"

Banks sat back in his chair and sighed. "Never."

"Then why should I start now?"

"So there's no way I can convince you to go into business with Mason Lou? He's about cocaine too, Nidia."

She smiled and allowed it to crawl into a slow glare. "Bad manors, Mr. Wales. Leave my home. And never ask me about him again." She wiped her mouth with the napkin and stormed away from the table.

CHAPTER THIRTY-NINE

Minnie was crying in her large princess style room when she heard a knock on her glass terrace door. Slowly she got up and opened it, only to reveal Arlyndo on the other side. Wearing a blue hoody and jeans he looked like a madman.

"Oh my god," she turned around and looked at her opened bedroom door. "How you get all the way up here?" She helped him inside, closed the terrace door and locked her bedroom door next. "Are you trying to get me killed or something? What if daddy saw you?"

"You look beautiful, Minnie," he said eyeing her pink nightgown. His breath smelling of hard core liquor.

"What are you doing here?"

"I can't be without you, Minnie."

She grabbed him and kissed his face and lips repeatedly because she missed him so much it burned. "I can't be without you either."

"Then why didn't you call me?" He yelled. "When you knew I was dying without you?"

"Please keep your voice down," she whispered.

"Fuck that!" He said louder. "I'm tired of niggas keeping us apart. You belong to me and—"

KNOCK! KNOCK! KNOCK!

The banging on the door caused Minnie's eyes to fly open. She was so scared she farted. "Get under the bed...please."

"Fuck that, I ain't—"

"Please..." She begged, on the verge of tears. The last thing she wanted was Banks to cave his chest in. "Don't do this."

Rolling his eyes, slowly he slithered under the bed.

KNOCK! KNOCK! KNOCK!

"Minnie, open the door," Banks yelled on the other side in the hallway. "I'm not fucking around!"

She took a deep breath and pulled it open, looking back once. "Hey, daddy." Her voice was sweet and innocent. It was a major difference from the *fuck you daddy's* he had become accustomed to around the house.

"Hey, daddy?" He said looking in the room from the doorway. "So you not mad at me anymore?"

"I'm really hurt but...I mean...what can I do?" She paused. "I'm just a kid."

"I know you don't see things my way right now." He paused. "And I know you're hurt, but everything I do is for you and the boys."

"Liar," Arlyndo said louder than he should have.

"What was that?" Banks frowned.

"Nothing, daddy," Minnie said, her heart rocking in her chest. "You know Harris be up late watching them science channels and stuff. You probably heard that from his room."

"Yeah..." Banks said suspiciously. "Maybe you're right." He took a deep breath. He was often a fool for her. "Listen, I want you to know I love you and that we're going to get this family where it should be." He grabbed her hands. "Trust me."

"I know."

He kissed her on the cheek. "Get dressed. I'll see you downstairs in a little bit."

"Ok, daddy."

When he walked away Arlyndo crawled from up under the bed. "What the fuck is he talking about?"

"You almost got me in trouble."

"Fuck that!" He yelled. "If you don't want me to scream you better tell the truth."

Minnie grabbed both of his hands and stared up at him. "We leaving."

"Leaving?" He said, his nostrils flaring. "What that mean?"

"Daddy bought an island and we leaving the country."

Hearing the news, Arlyndo felt gut punched and flopped on the edge of her bed to catch his breath. He would be a maniac without her. "But you...you can't leave."

"I know, but it's nothing I can do about it." She shrugged.

Arlyndo reached behind his back and grabbed his gun. Slowly he aimed the barrel in her direction, right about her chin. "If you leave I'll fucking kill you. Do you hear me?" He pointed the gun to his head. "I'll kill you and kill me too!" He pointed it back at her. "I swear to God I will!"

"Arlyndo, don't—"

"I'm serious, Minnie! I can't...I can't..." Defeated, the gun dropped to the bed and he pulled her between his legs, breathing into her stomach. "You gotta tell him he can't leave." He looked up at her, tears in his eyes. "You gotta do whatever you gotta to stop him. Don't let him take you away from me. Please."

Tops sat in the car in the parking lot of the small pavilion, which was hosting Mason's art show. Since the event was underground, because of the nature of his bloody work, it was initially hard to get a ticket. But after some time he was able to pay a man ten stacks to gain entry.

The event had gone on for over an hour and although Mason's creations had been flying off the walls, he was nowhere in sight. When he finally pulled

By T. STYLES

up in a dark blue Rolls Royce, he called Linden. "He's here! Finally!"

"Good," Linden said. "The moment he steps out put one in his head. If he moves a little after that hit him again."

"You got it."

Mason was just about to step out of the car when his phone rang. When he saw the number on the screen he was shocked. Placing his car in park he hit the button and answered the call. "Hey...I..."

"What you doing?" Banks asked in a low voice.

"Nothing for real," he said, despite having an entire room full of creeps waiting to meet the man with the bloody art. "But listen, I wanted to apologize for...I mean...."

"I know."

"I'm serious, man." Mason continued. "I should've respected your wishes and not pushed shit with our kids. But we been cool for too long, Banks. I ain't trying to do this all over again with you."

"Me either." Banks sighed. "So what you doing tonight?"

Mason looked at the pavilion and the many cars waiting in the parking lot for him. "Like I said, nothing for real." He lied.

"Good, come over for dinner. Tonight. Bring the boys."

Mason put his car in drive. "On my way."

Confused, Tops looked at Mason backing out of the parking lot. He called Linden back. "The nigga leaving!"

"What?" Linden yelled. "Are you sure?"

"I know a nigga leaving when I see one." Tops focused on Mason's Rolls Royce driving away. "Maybe he's on to me."

"Whatever you do keep eyes on him." Linden continued. "Don't let him out your sight."

"I'm on it!" Tops put his car into drive and followed his trail.

By T. STYLES

CHAPTER FORTY

The wait staff removed sterling silver plates as they prepared for dessert for the Wales and the Lou families at Banks' mansion. After being invited back, The Lou's were hopeful that the youngest members of the organization hadn't fucked them out of a connection with The Plug, and so they were on their best behavior.

Suits, ties and slick bottoms.

While the two families carried on as if nothing were happening, Minnie and Arlyndo sat at the table heated. Both knowing that this was possibly the last meal the families would share together.

"I want to make a toast," Mason said happily. He grabbed his glass and rose to his feet. "Everybody pick up whatever is in front of you."

Everyone complied.

"I know we almost had a set back," Mason continued. Looking at Minnie and Arlyndo. "But I'm glad that like always the Wales and the Lou's could put it back together." He paused. "And I know that this is just the beginning, but we're going to be stronger for it."

"Are you sure about that?" Minnie asked with her arms crossed over her body. "I mean, how do you *really* know?"

"Shut up, Minnie," Spacey said.

"Don't tell my girl to shut up!" Arlyndo yelled. "I'm tired of ya'll acting like we too young to say stuff 'round here."

"Son...relax," Mason said to Arlyndo.

"You gonna tell your friend or do you want me?" Arlyndo asked Banks.

Banks glared, confused on what he was saying. Besides, he had specifically forbidden Minnie from saying anything about them moving, so surely she couldn't have overstepped her boundaries that quickly. Besides, her phone had been taken and guards stayed on her twenty-four-seven.

"Lyndo, how 'bout whatever you got on your chest we talk about later," Banks said feeling he might know after all. "In private."

"You ain't answer the question, Big Boss," Arlyndo said slyly. "You want me to tell my pops or do you wanna tell him?"

Mason glared. "What's going on, Banks?"

Banks took a deep breath. "I wanted to tell you but not today. Not like this."

"Tell me what?" Mason frowned.

"Me and my family out."

Mason squeezed the glass in his hand. "What that mean? You out?"

"We done with this shit, man," Banks said. "I been telling you forever that there ain't no future in this cocaine life. So I gotta get my family out of here while I still can." He paused. "And that work I gave you...or Bet gave you rather...you can keep that. It's paid for already. Consider it a parting gift."

"But what about us?" Howard said. "You gonna leave us out here on our dicks because you want out the coke game?"

"I got to take care of my family."

"But what about us?" Mason repeated trembling. "Ain't we family too?"

"Mason, let's talk about this in private," Banks continued. "Away from the kids."

"Nah...we can talk—"

Suddenly a bullet ripped through the glass Mason was holding in his hand, causing his palm to open up like butter. It had entered from the window but Mason, thinking Wales members were about to assassinate him, every Lou in attendance removed their weapons from their hips and fired in the Wales' direction.

"It's a set up!" Mason yelled firing at Banks and his family.

The Wales, having prepared for this before, all dropped to the floor and grabbed the weapons that were secured from up under the table. Hearing the gunplay in session, Wales soldiers poured into the dining room and busted at Mason and his spawn. Bullet after bullet crisscrossed the dining room ripping into everything. The chandeliers...glasses and walls.

Feeling outnumbered, the Lou's went running for the exit but the Wales soldiers were relentless and on their trail.

More bullets hit the windows, the others hit the doors and before long the Wales family was helped into the secret hiding place by the soldiers. Ten minutes later, hidden behind the wall in the library, Banks and his family waited for the call from their most trusted man...Stretch.

Feeling stupid as fuck, Minnie cried softly into Spacey's chest while the others paced.

Fifteen minutes later Banks' cell rang. "What's up?" He said.

"Banks, it's Stretch."

His family looked at him with wide eyes.

"What's going on?" Banks asked. "Them niggas out my house?"

His family members crowded him.

"Yes. The coast is clear," Stretch said.

"Anybody got hit?" Banks asked.

"Yeah...Derrick." He paused. "It's bad too. He may be dead."

By T. STYLES

Tops paced in a dark alley behind a liquor store, waiting on Linden with a huge smile on his face. When he finally pulled up he rushed over to his red Ram pickup truck, heavy with some news. "What happened?" Linden asked from the driver's seat.

Tops approached the passenger's window and talked through it. "Mason went to Banks house and I followed."

"How you get on the property with all those soldiers?"

"They weren't guarding the land. All were inside. I guess they expected something may go down tonight." He paused. "Anyway, I hopped a gate, walked around back and peered through the dining room window. When I saw Mason standing there I took a shot."

"What happened though?" He asked with wide eyes. The anticipation was killing him. "You get Mason or not?"

Tops smiled. "No...but it's better."

"What could be better than that?"

"I hit the glass Mason was holding and they started firing at each other instead," Tops continued. "Banks and Mason." He laughed. "I'm not sure but I think we just started another war."

Smiling, when Linden's phone rang he looked down and saw an unfamiliar number. He threw up one finger to silence Tops. "Who this?"

"Linden, it's Mason!"

Linden glared and sat back in his seat. He hadn't heard his brother's voice in over twenty years. "What you want?"

"You were right about that nigga, man. You were so fucking right."

Linden grinned and winked at Tops. "What happened?" He asked as if he didn't know.

"Can you be at my house in an hour?" He yelled. "I'm having a meeting and I'll tell you everything you wanna know."

Linden rubbed his hands together and grinned. "I'm on my way."

Bank's Mansion

"Why would you do that?" Banks asked Minnie as he paced the living room floor looking down at her. His family was also present and all wanted an answer from the brat.

She was a mess and snot ran down her face as she cried heavily. "I...I...I was...mad. Mad you were gonna take me away from Arlyndo. Because I love him. I fucking love him so much, daddy!"

"Minnie, you were wrong!" Bet yelled. "And you have no idea what you've done! No idea at all!"

By T. STYLES

"I hate everybody!" Minnie got up and ran into her room.

"Stay with her," Banks told one of his soldiers. "And if she closes the door break it down. Don't let her out your sight."

The man nodded and followed Minnie.

Banks looked at Bet, Spacey, Joey and Harris and took a deep breath. "There is no turning back now," he said. "I know Mason. More than any of you in this room. And we've been here before." He paused. "The only difference now is that we got kids and...more to lose." Banks wiped his hand down his face. "God forbid Derrick dies." He felt his pressure rising. "Grab your personal documents and anything that's important like pictures. Don't worry about your clothes and things like that...I bought everybody a new wardrobe." He paused. "We leaving tomorrow."

Mason's Trap House

Mason stood in front of his family in the living room of his trap house in rage. His hand was covered with a bloodied bandage. Just like Banks, Mason had men on guard around his property and in the house. Everyone was on high alert and a doctor was in the back seeing about Derrick but the state of his survival looked grim. This didn't do anything but enrage Mason even more.

In attendance were Jersey, Howard, Patterson, Linden and even Garret, the man who recently went behind his back to make a deal with Banks. The dude was foul but Mason figured for the war ahead of him, he needed everyone who despised the boss to some degree on his squad. A few of Mason's low-level soldiers were also in attendance.

The living room was packed.

And all were on edge.

Mason took a deep breath. "Banks crossed the line." He paused wielding a tight fist. "And it's my fault for trusting him. But there is something I want to tell you, something that will...that may...it may make things more understandable."

"We listening, Pops." Howard said.

Wales' Mansion

Stretch stood in the basement bathroom with Bet who was crying uncontrollably. He had his hands on both of her shoulders and squeezed them as he looked

By T. STYLES

into her eyes. "I don't mean to make you cry but why didn't you tell me about this shit?"

"Because it wasn't my place," Bet sobbed softly.

"So what you expect me to do?" Stretch continued. "Just allow you to take my kids away from me?"

She pushed him backwards. "Your kids? Your fucking kids?"

"Yes...*my* kids," he said through clenched teeth. "When I agreed to...to help you and Banks have children I never thought...I never thought I wouldn't lay eyes on them again."

"But Banks said he wanted you to go with us. To the island."

"Well he didn't tell me."

When someone opened the door, Bet and Stretch separated from each other.

"What's going on?" Spacey asked with wide eyes. He had walked into the bathroom and into a conversation that was so astounding it was making him dizzy. "You our...our father?"

Bet covered her mouth with both hands. This was the worst case scenario. "Oh my god no. No."

Stretch walked up to him. "Spacey, please...you can't...you can't tell anybody about—

Spacey removed his weapon from his back and pointed the barrel in his direction. "You coming with me!"

Stretch threw his hands up. "Please don't—"

"Now!"

Mason's Trap House

Mason paced the room faster as he continued to tell the history of his and Banks' relationship. Everyone was on edge as they waited for him to finish.

"We know you knew him as a kid, pops," Howard said. "You gotta tell us something else now."

Mason took a deep breath. He never thought about telling this secret and yet here he was about to reveal it all. He had plans to take it to his grave. "I met Banks in elementary school and she was my first girlfriend."

Everybody frowned thinking Mason had the game fucked up.

Even the soldiers who were there strictly for protection couldn't help but gasp.

"You not making sense," Linden said. "You high?"

"Just listen," he paused. "Banks and I met in elementary school. Her father was trying to find her a boyfriend because he said his daughter was too...boyish." He took a deep breath. "But I was young and ain't like nobody really, so I got with her. She was so nice. So easy to talk to and I started to care about her for real. I knew I was a kid but still. But when we

By T. STYLES

got to middle school stuff started changing. When she came to my house, she started sneaking my hats and stuffing her hair inside them and shit like that. Posing like a boy in the mirror. I thought it was a joke but after that she started wearing my shoes because we wore the same size."

"What the fuck...," Linden said under his breath.

"Dennis and his moms pretty much thought she'd get over it until she tried to kill herself. Jumped off a bridge by the house. Broke her back and had to stay out of school for one year."

Banks' Mansion

Standing in his office, Banks couldn't believe Spacey was holding a gun on Stretch and at the same time he knew he had to come clean with everything, even though he was certain it would destroy all he built.

Bet, Spacey and Stretch looked at him, hoping he would make everything make sense.

Mainly for the boy.

"Son, put the gun down," Banks pleaded.

"No!" Spacey continued, still waving it at Stretch. "I wanna know...I wanna know what's going on right now!"

"Son...put the gun—"

"RIGHT FUCKING NOW!" Spacey continued, now aiming the .45 at Banks.

Afraid he was about to shoot the love of her life in the face, she jumped in front of her husband. "Spacey, no!" Bet said, palms in her son's direction. "Please don't—"

"Shhhh." Banks said pushing her softly aside. Focusing back on Spacey he walked up to him and smiled. Slowly he raised a hand, grabbed the barrel and pulled it out of his shaky grasp.

Immediately Stretch took the weapon and Spacey cried in Banks' arms.

When Spacey was calmer, he sat him down on the sofa and took a deep breath. Sitting on the edge of his desk, Banks looked down at the young man who bared his last name. This was going to be rough and for support; Bet sat next to Spacey and grabbed his hand.

On the other hand, feeling things were too intense, due to the shit he caused, Stretch was about to walk out.

"Nah, man...stay," Banks told him.

"You sure?" Stretch asked.

Banks nodded yes.

Stretch leaned up against the door.

Tears began to fill Banks' eyes as he came clean with the one thing he never wanted to face. A secret that he not only kept close to his heart with only Bet, Stretch and Mason knowing the truth, but also a secret that was his number two reason for wanting to leave the country, for fear it might come out. Or if he got locked up and he was sent to a woman's prison.

"Spacey, I'm a...I was...born a woman."

Spacey's eyes widened. "What...I don't...I don't understand."

Banks wiped his tears away and took a deep breath. "I was born a woman but all my life...all my fucking life I always felt like...like that wasn't me. Like God got it wrong or something."

Spacey frowned. "But the kids...we...you don't have titties." He pointed at his chest.

"I had surgery when I was in my early twenties." He took a deep breath. "And removed them then. I got the scars for it though."

"So...so you got a dick too?"

"No...no, son." He paused. "I don't."

"I'm not your fucking son!" Spacey yelled. "Remember? That's the whole point!"

"Spacey...please," Bet said. "Don't talk to him that way. Try to listen."

Spacey looked down at his trembling fingers. "But you always look like..." He pointed at Banks' crotch. "You got a bulge."

"It's a..."

"A fucking dildo?" Spacey said, trying not to cry harder. "Are you serious? Am I on some trick show?" He looked around. "What about the hair? On your face?"

"Hormone...hormone replacement therapy." Banks stuttered. "I been taking it for years." He paused. "I just want you to know that me being born a woman has nothing to do with—"

"Are we your kids or not?"

"Of course you are," Bet said.

"I want the fuckin' truth!" Spacey yelled. "None of this fake playing house shit anymore. The truth! Please!"

Silence.

Banks took a deep breath. "You, Joey and Harris are not my...not my biological children. And I, I had one of my eggs removed so your mother..." He took a deep breath. "Your mother carried it and that's how Minnie was born. She is my blood."

Devastated, Spacey laughed and cried at the same time. "All my life I tried to get closer to you. To prove to you that I deserved your love instead of Minnie and her disloyal ass and you..." He shook his head. "And now it all makes sense." He got up and walked toward the door.

Banks followed him. "Spacey, please don't—"

"Just leave me the fuck alone!" He pointed at Banks. "Do you hear me? Leave me the fuck alone!" He ran out the door.

Mason's Trap House

"This shit makes so much sense," Linden said to himself.

"Not to me," Howard said. "I mean, I hear him saying that Unc is a woman...or was a woman, but does that make Pops gay?"

"How you sound, nigga?" Patterson said. "Dad's far from gay."

"Let me finish," Mason said. "She kept saying she didn't feel like herself inside and her parents made a decision, to let her live like she wanted. As a boy. But that meant changing schools. So she could have a fresh start. So that's what they did, after she broke her back." He paused. "I guess after some time she changed her name from Blakeslee to Banks and when she was old enough, Dennis put her on hormone therapy." He paused. "But it was hard for me at first because I still fucked with her. Still looked at her like a girl, until she cut her hair and told me if I kept trying...like to kiss her and shit like that, then...we would be done."

"So you had feelings for her...maybe even up to recently?" Jersey asked with wide eyes.

Silence.

Jersey ran in the back of the house, upset and crying.

"What the fuck is really going on?" Linden said under his breath, wiping a hand down his face.

"Dad, what does this mean?" Howard said. "Because I'm so fucking confused right now."

"I'm telling you this...this secret because I want you to know how serious I am. The only person who knows about this is me, Bet, Banks and Stretch. And now ya'll do too."

"But how...I mean...the kids...the...I'm confused," Linden said.

"None of that matters. I kept his secret for as long as I'm willing to do." He paused. "Now what I do know is this...he won't get on that plane." He cocked his gun. "Not alive anyway."

FCI LOW - DORM
PRESENT DAY - CHRISTMAS EVE

The prisoners looked at Tops and inmate #11578, who was now not moving on the floor. The story rocked every man in attendance. "So you tried to kill Mason Lou?" Byrd asked Tops. "Are you fucking serious?" He laughed.

"I tried to do much more before that," Tops said, glaring down at the injured inmate.

"So who is that nigga?" Byrd continued. "You gotta tell us now."

Tops looked over at Kirk. "Why don't you ask this nigga right here? He knows...don't you, *Kirk*?"

Kirk glared.

Everyone focused on Kirk now.

"Yeah, I'm not the only one who got a story to tell about this family." Tops laughed. "Ain't that right?"

Kirk shrugged.

"Can ya'll tell us what's going on?" Byrd asked more irritated than anything. "I'm tired of the games."

Kirk's jaw twitched. "The nigga on the floor is Linden Lou," he said. "And I'm Harris Kirk Wales. And I did my best to off this bitch ass nigga in private. Paid for it and everything." He sighed. "Somebody did it earlier than ordered though." He kicked #11578 in the gut.

"But you were about to run and tell—"

"I ain't want the shit to come back to me because me and this nigga got history," Kirk said, cutting Byrd off.

"So you were gonna put it on us instead?" Byrd continued.

Silence.

"Man...it's not like that." He looked at Tops. "But there's more to the story then what Tops is telling you. And this time you gotta hear it from me."

COMING SOON...

WAR 2: ALL HELL BREAKS LOOSE

THANKSGIVING EVE 2018

The Cartel Publications Order Form

www.thecartelpublications.com

Inmates **ONLY** receive novels for $10.00 per book **PLUS** shipping fee **PER BOOK.**

(Mail Order **MUST** come from inmate directly to receive discount)

Shyt List 1	_____	$15.00
Shyt List 2	_____	$15.00
Shyt List 3	_____	$15.00
Shyt List 4	_____	$15.00
Shyt List 5	_____	$15.00
Pitbulls In A Skirt	_____	$15.00
Pitbulls In A Skirt 2	_____	$15.00
Pitbulls In A Skirt 3	_____	$15.00
Pitbulls In A Skirt 4	_____	$15.00
Pitbulls In A Skirt 5	_____	$15.00
Victoria's Secret	_____	$15.00
Poison 1	_____	$15.00
Poison 2	_____	$15.00
Hell Razor Honeys	_____	$15.00
Hell Razor Honeys 2	_____	$15.00
A Hustler's Son	_____	$15.00
A Hustler's Son 2	_____	$15.00
Black and Ugly	_____	$15.00
Black and Ugly As Ever	_____	$15.00
Ms Wayne & The Queens of DC **(LGBT)**	_____	$15.00
Black And The Ugliest	_____	$15.00
Year Of The Crackmom	_____	$15.00
Deadheads	_____	$15.00
The Face That Launched A Thousand Bullets	_____	$15.00
The Unusual Suspects	_____	$15.00
Paid In Blood	_____	$15.00
Raunchy	_____	$15.00
Raunchy 2	_____	$15.00
Raunchy 3	_____	$15.00
Mad Maxxx (4th Book Raunchy Series)	_____	$15.00
Quita's Dayscare Center	_____	$15.00
Quita's Dayscare Center 2	_____	$15.00
Pretty Kings	_____	$15.00
Pretty Kings 2	_____	$15.00
Pretty Kings 3	_____	$15.00
Pretty Kings 4	_____	$15.00
Silence Of The Nine	_____	$15.00
Silence Of The Nine 2	_____	$15.00
Silence Of The Nine 3	_____	$15.00
Prison Throne	_____	$15.00
Drunk & Hot Girls	_____	$15.00
Hersband Material **(LGBT)**	_____	$15.00
The End: How To Write A Bestselling Novel In 30 Days (Non-Fiction Guide)	_____	$15.00
Upscale Kittens	_____	$15.00
Wake & Bake Boys	_____	$15.00
Young & Dumb	_____	$15.00
Young & Dumb 2: Vyce's Getback	_____	$15.00

By T. STYLES

Tranny 911 **(LGBT)** _____	$15.00
Tranny 911: Dixie's Rise **(LGBT)** _____	$15.00
First Comes Love, Then Comes Murder _____	$15.00
Luxury Tax _____	$15.00
The Lying King _____	$15.00
Crazy Kind Of Love _____	$15.00
Goon _____	$15.00
And They Call Me God _____	$15.00
The Ungrateful Bastards _____	$15.00
Lipstick Dom **(LGBT)** _____	$15.00
A School of Dolls **(LGBT)** _____	$15.00
Hoetic Justice _____	$15.00
KALI: Raunchy Relived _____	$15.00
(5th Book in Raunchy Series)	
Skeezers _____	$15.00
Skeezers 2 _____	$15.00
You Kissed Me, Now I Own You _____	$15.00
Nefarious _____	$15.00
Redbone 3: The Rise of The Fold _____	$15.00
The Fold (4th Redbone Book) _____	$15.00
Clown Niggas _____	$15.00
The One You Shouldn't Trust _____	$15.00
The WHORE The Wind	
Blew My Way _____	$15.00
She Brings The Worst Kind _____	$15.00
The House That Crack Built _____	$15.00
The House That Crack Built 2 _____	$15.00
The House That Crack Built 3 _____	$15.00
The House That Crack Built 4 _____	$15.00
Level Up **(LGBT)** _____	$15.00
Villains: It's Savage Season _____	$15.00
Gay For My Bae _____	$15.00
War _____	$15.00

(**Redbone 1 & 2** are **NOT** Cartel Publications novels and if **ordered** the cost is **FULL** price of $15.00 **each. No Exceptions**.)

Please add $5.00 **PER BOOK** for shipping and handling. **Inmates** too!

The Cartel Publications * P.O. BOX 486 OWINGS MILLS MD 21117

Name: _____

Address: _____

City/State: _____

Contact/Email: _____

Please allow 7-10 BUSINESS days before shipping.
The Cartel Publications is NOT responsible for Prison Orders rejected!

NO RETURNS and NO REFUNDS
NO PERSONAL CHECKS ACCEPTED
STAMPS NO LONGER ACCEPTED

WAR

CPSIA information can be obtained
at www.ICGtesting.com
Printed in the USA
LVHW111516180119
604418LV00001B/91/P

9 781948 373227